FEAR:

Of the Water

Sirens Call Publications

FEAR: Of the Water

FEAR: Of the Water

Vena Cava
SL Schmitz…………………………………….... **3**

Clear Water
Kerry G.S. Lipp…………………………….... **27**

Chlorine
Blaise Torrance………………………………. **45**

Payment
Brent Abell……………………………………... **61**

The Iceberg
Patrick Van Slyke……………………………. **81**

Moon in Submergence
Timothy C. Hobbs………………………….... **101**

Rain, Rain, Go Away! *Please…*
Vincent Bivona………………………………. **133**

And The River Rolled
Connor Rice…………………………………... **153**

The *Rose-Marie*
Jon Olson…………………………….….... **185**

Pool Closed
Shenoa Carroll-Bradd………………………... **213**

The Flood
Justin M. Ryan………………………………. **231**

Crème Filling
Zachary O'Shea……………………………..... **245**

About the Authors………………………….... **261**

Sirens Call Publications

Sirens Call Publications

Vena Cava

SL Schmitz

I move quickly through my evening rounds, always accompanied by Carmen. We have developed a routine, a system of sorts, which keeps us from lingering too long at the bedsides of the coherent or the sane. Carmen approaches the bed first in order to engage the patient in conversation, a way of checking lucidity while peering into their eyes. I watch, listening, making swift but firm judgment calls based on my observations. If the person is not in crisis, or if the bleeding is not too severe, we move on.

It is not long before we reach the prone body of a young girl. She is lying on a mattress on the floor, one of her broken legs carelessly splayed over the side. She is unresponsive to Carmen's murmurings, her eyes glazed and unflinching despite the flies buzzing around the corners of her dry mouth, her broken nose. There is a gaping wound on her collarbone, pus and dark blood pooling around the deep contusion on her head. Her situation is grim, but she will go on living for an unspecified period of time as long as we force her to drink water and start her on antibiotics to fend off infection. Unfortunately, we have precious little of either resource.

"They brought her in last night. Someone found her lying in a street in Tent City and carried her to the gates. She has no name, and no one has claimed her," Carmen told me in a low voice. Her tone was soft, sad. "One of the guards brought her up."

"We'll wait a day or two, see what happens," I say, careful not to touch the filthy sheets. The girl's breathing is ragged, and fresh blood is oozing from her head wound. I hope she dies quietly in the night, with minimal pain. It is the best any of us can hope for these days.

We move slowly, careful not to step on any of the bodies lying all around us. What is left of the hospital has been dragged to higher ground; we have located as much equipment as could be salvaged from the water and carried it up to the fourth and fifth floors of the remaining medical building. The mattresses scattered all over the floor filled so quickly with the sick and suffering that we have been forced to turn people away.

Carmen leans over an ancient woman, brushes her fingers over the paper thin flesh of her forehead. "Agatha," she is whispering, tapping her wrist. There is no response. The nurse turns to me, her words brief and clinical. "She has been this way for six days, either completely unconscious or else screaming in agony. She is a diabetic, and the wound on her side has become gangrenous."

I nod. I have already made my decision. I hold out one of my hands, no longer caring about the dirt embedded under my nails. I haven't washed my hands in clean water in over a week, and I can't remember the last time I bathed. We are rationing the baby wipes, only using them for surgery. I do not have to say anything to my assistant – we have completed this gruesome activity too many times before to engage in comment or opinion. It is for the best that we do what we must do, and not dwell.

Carmen looks down at the small silver dish in her hands and takes off the cover, reverentially holding out the contents for me to administer. I sigh, but it is a very tiny sigh, not something that anybody else would hear.

"Ready?" I say, frustrated with my lack of tools, the unpleasantness of the situation. This has to be done manually.

One of the few remaining staff goes and fetches me the materials I will need; a slim rubber tube and a cup with just a few precious drops of water in it. I take one of the sugar-cubes from the silver dish and dissolve it in the water. Slowly, with great care, I snake the tube down the woman's throat, making sure not to trigger a gag reflex. Carmen pours the sugar slurry into the tube, all the while stroking the woman's creased forehead as if she were soothing a crying baby. We have become experts in this grim exercise; between the two of us, we manage to get enough of the liquid into the woman's digestive system, and then we fade back from the body. Two attendants immediately come forward, one to hold the her hand and one to sit on the other side, touching her face and whispering into her good ear, the one that has not been crushed. Although our tools to alleviate the suffering are few, we still believe in compassion and take great pains to usher the dying into the next world with as much dignity as possible. My nurse and I do not even pause; together, we move on to the next bed, the next immobile body, Carmen taking great care to replace the top on the silver dish to prevent any of the moistened sugar cubes from falling out. That was the seventeenth patient we have fed a sugar-cube to tonight.

The hospital is recognized as the last remaining attempt to maintain a sense of law in the destroyed city. In order to keep control of the desperate crowds of people gathered just outside the gates, we have kept only one stairwell open; everything else has been boarded up. There are guards posted at the bottom of the stairs, and guards at the barbed wire gates of the hospital. They are loyal to us, because we pay each of them with a liter of clean water a day. We have the last working generators in the whole region, and the only time we turn them on is to light our stoves to boil water in the huge pots from the cafeteria. We ran out of bleach and iodine within the first two weeks, and our homemade solar water sterilizers have not been as effective as hoped.

There is no electricity, no petrol, and no known food storages left in any of the parishes still above water. Our smart-phones and laptops worked for a few weeks after the first earthquake, but little by little the power grids and internet began to fail. With no electricity to recharge the electronics, we gradually lost touch with the outside world. When the second set of earthquakes came, along with the tidal waves and tsunamis around the globe, social media and the internet cloud became silent. We came to the reluctant conclusion that the broadband still existed, that transmission was still possible, but that there were too few left alive and no resources left to use it. The world had gone silent. The thought was not comforting.

Our levees are going to collapse soon. Already, water is beginning to seep over the canals and flood the streets closest to the ports. Every day, the ocean rises and comes closer to us, towards the ten-thousand or more people huddled under makeshift shelters, bringing with it malaria and dysentery. They have come here because we are the last vestige of civilization - the hospital and the great Catholic cathedral up the street are the only two buildings that somehow survived the damage. The people have grown ragged and thin, many are collapsing from lack of water and food. At first, our wards were full of head injuries, broken bodies, weeping sores and massive blunt trauma, but with the passing of six weeks and then seven, our patients have thinned out to a few hundred tragic cases.

We have no bandages, no antibiotics, and no pain medications left. There is nothing to give the people to comfort them in their agony, nothing left to prevent the madness and hysteria caused by the unrelieved suffering. There are two doctors, eight nurses, a few nuns and missionaries, a handful of volunteers to serve as orderlies, and a small group of dedicated housekeeping staff to run these wards.

And a small silver dish full of cyanide-laced sugar cubes.

Night-time is the worst time of all. When I look out of the cracked windows of the fourth floor, I can see the crowds milling outside the perimeter, the fights breaking out, the crying children and the faint glow from the solar-powered lights. There is no law and order down there- it has become every man for himself. I rub my dirty hands against my temples, knowing that even with severe rationing, the hospital only has enough food to last another fifteen days. After that, we will have no option but to abandon the city and try to make our way out into the open country. I am dreading the thought of leaving the safety of the medical building, but we are running out of choices.

***

I am shaken awake by Carmen. She and I share a small storage closet beside one of the old waiting rooms; it is cramped but tolerable living quarters. Carmen is the more prepared of the two of us, sleeping with a loaded pistol under her pillow. It makes me feel safe, knowing that she is armed and ready for any disaster. We have grown so close, so dependent on one another since that fateful day when we met on the highway. "Mercedes!" she says urgently, shaking me again. "Come on – something is going on downstairs. You need to hurry!"

I follow her into the waiting room, towards one of the windows. Peering down, we see a group of approximately thirty people, some standing and some kneeling in the ankle-deep water that now covers most of the low lying areas. They all seem to be staring at the same thing, an object that is directly below us and not visible from our vantage point; I can't be sure, but it looked like some of them were praying.

"How did those people get past the guards?" is my first question. Like it or not, I have assumed the role of leader of this hospital and protector of all those within its walls. I am concerned that the praying group has not been chased away by our contingency of selected guardsmen -- it is only when I look more closely that I realize that several of the people are our own guards. My eyes follow the stagnant water towards the locked and chained hospital gates and it is there that I realize for the first time that the crowds are still, silent, staring in the same direction as the small group below. I feel a chill on the back of my neck, an old warning sign that something is not right, a childhood foreshadowing that a dark and malignant fear has manifested itself and become solid. "I'm going down there," I say, heading for the stairwell.

"No, Mercedes, don't!" a chorus of voices reaches out to me, drawing me back. "It's not a good idea," a nurse added. "They know who you are."

I turn to them, confused. "Who am I?" I asked, searching their faces for an answer.

The words hang in the air, drawing all of the oxygen and light out of the room. I stare at them, a group of haggard medical personnel wearing scrubs that haven't been washed since the first earthquakes hit. Some of us have sores, wounds that won't heal, infections and coughs. It is only a matter of time before gangrene claims a leg here, an arm there. We are exhausted, ghosts, surrounded by the sobs of weak and dehydrated patients.

"There are stories being told… some people are speaking up against the hospital. Against you," a young woman whispered. She is one of the volunteers, working day and night to keep order in the wards.

There are unspoken words floating in the air. I know what they are all thinking. I have heard the accusations, too.

"We know it's not true," a nun said, spreading her hands as if to comfort all of us. "The people are confused. Everything is so terrible now, and old stories get new life in times of great trouble." She paused, looking nervously around the room.

"Some of them are calling you La Lechusa, come back to haunt the earth," one of the attendants said, not meeting my gaze. "Because… because of so many dead."

"But," Carmen stepped forward as if to shield me from their words. "The people know how hard Dr. Castiblanco is working, how many of their lives she has saved. When all of the other doctors ran away, everyone knows that she and Dr. Duarte stayed."

"They also know about the sugar cubes," Dr. Duarte added in a sepulcher tone.

"Does she look like an owl?" Carmen's voice became uncharacteristically shrill, angry.

"We never see her at night. She lives in the closet, with you," the attendant replied softly.

I open my mouth, but no sound comes out. There is a rush of emotions, a mixture of sorrow, shame, despair, and hopelessness. I reach out to grasp a wall, and almost fall to the floor. Carmen steadies me; we have been through so much together. I remember meeting her for the first time, in those first hours after the world crumbled apart. She was sitting on the side of the road with her husband's body in her arms, head down, defeated. I had just crawled out of a ditch from which my car and a dozen others had crashed and caught fire. Limping and dazed, I think I was the only survivor from the wreck. "I'm a doctor," I said to her, sitting beside her, praying that the earth would not move again and swallow us whole. I looked at the mass of blood and twisted bones in her arms. "Maybe I can help."

"I'm a nurse," she replied flatly. "He's dead." We sat together for several hours without speaking, than quietly agreed to walk together towards the hospital. Perhaps, we had thought back then, we could be of help to others.

Now they call me a witch – a soul stealer. Just for wanting to decrease suffering. I bit my lip, an old habit from my youth, then I made my decision.

"I'm going down to see what's going on," I told them in the clearest, calmest voice that I could muster.

"Alright," Carmen put a hand reassuringly on my shoulder. "I'll come with you."

It reminded me of our hushed conversations after we heard about the tsunamis that had devastated Japan and Australia, the month-long rains and tornadoes pelting the Americas. There were rumors that a great ocean trench had opened in the middle of the Pacific, sucking vast amounts of the saltwater into the earth and then spewing it out to destroy whole civilizations. Every day, more and more people arrived at the avenue outside of our hospital, bringing their comatose grandmothers and their children with flesh hanging off of their bones, their search for sanctuary and their prayers for salvation. They were coming towards the ocean instead of away from it, drawn by the hope that a crumbling medical building and a collapsing church might somehow save them. When the last of our smartphones and computers went dead, we lost communication with the rest of the world. We have no idea what is going on outside of our own dirty windows.

And the sick and the injured keep coming. Endless broken bodies, with no way left to stop the pain. Helpless and alone, Carmen and I had reluctantly agreed to build our boat to cross the River Styx. We had nothing to pay the ferryman except a bit of poison, understanding what we were capable of doing and knowing that it must be done. *First, do no harm.*

***

We walked the four flights down to the ground as quickly as we could. We were surprised when we reached the barrier and found only three guards on duty; our agreement with the group of men we had hired was to guarantee our safety at all costs. There was never supposed to be less than twenty men at the barrier at all times, thirty at the gates. We stepped into the dim sunlight, shielding our eyes and looking around until we focused on the people clumped around one of the side areas of the hospital entranceway. As we made our way towards the group, the only sound we could hear was our ankles sloshing in the water. The silent crowd outside the barricade and circling the entire cul-de-sac of the hospital campus were watching us with hungry eyes. Then, the rumblings began.

"La Lechusa," we could hear faintly. "That is her – the witch!" "I've seen her flying over our heads at night!" "La Madonna!" A song floats towards us, softly at first and then stronger as more voices join. They are singing hymns. "It is Dr. Castiblanco, come down to save us!" "La Madre…"

Carmen and I glance at one another. She raises her chin to me, a signal to keep moving forward. We join the kneeling women, guards, children, and the one surviving Catholic priest, craning our necks to see the attraction.

At first, all I see is an altar fashioned out of a piece of wood and some rocks. There are soggy stuffed animals, articles of worn and tattered toddler's clothing, bright pieces of ribbons, and a few precious candles. A litter of past lives, lost loves. Among the many photographs and handwritten notes, there is a multitude of bird carcasses. It is unsettling to see so many dead birds scattered all over the ground, rotten and full of maggots. I wonder if the birds represent pagan sacrifices at the foot of the Catholic altar until I realize that these offerings have been pushed up against the concrete of the building. People are looking upwards, not to the heavens but to something closer. Their eyes are fixated on the side of the building. I follow their gaze, and it takes me a few moments to orient myself, to focus on the image.

The two-story high black glass-panels are the only remaining walls of glass left on the whole building. There, stretching across eight panels of windows the sun was shining in such a way that I could see the distinct outline of the rainbow-colored apparition of a woman's face. It was tall, very tall, and I could easily see the features of her head, her veil, her torso, two open hands piously reaching up to the heavens. Shocked, we moved closer. The sun was glinting off the reflective panes, and the vision shimmered in the rising heat. I swallowed, looking around for something, anything that could explain the appearance of this watery visage, but nothing stood out as obvious. The unmistakable vision of Mary gazed out upon the encampment of desperate survivors, offering a sign, a promise that all had been forgiven, forgotten.

As I shuffled towards the apparition, I could feel fingers reaching for the hem of my scrubs, brushing against my arms and touching my hair, as if I were made of feathers that could be stroked and plucked. People were making way for me, parting for me to cross between them. I am both humbled and frightened by their attention. The Priest came forward and held out his hand to me. "Dr. Castiblanco," he said in a booming voice with great ceremony. "We are so glad to see you today, helping us welcome the arrival of our Mother Mary!"

"Dr. Castiblanco, Dr. Castiblanco" the crowd shifts, everyone trying to get a good look at me. "She is blessed… she is evil… she is here… she will take care of us…" The song continues, voices lifting into the heat of the day, the humidity of the ocean.

"That is real, isn't it Father?" I breathe, pointing to the apparition. I am barely able to control my emotions.

"Oh, it is real alright!" He beamed, firmly grasping my arm and leading me forward. "She has come in our hour of need. She has come to save us!" He grabs me, and before I can stop him he begins pulling me away from the enormous vision, shouting the whole time. He is taking me further away from the safety of the hospital, towards the gates where the crowd has begun cheering and clapping and chanting my name.

Holding me tightly, he drags me towards Tent City, the voices clamoring for me, for my healing powers, for my hands to be laid on the sick, for Santa Mercedes to come and touch their heads, their wounds, make the hunger and thirst and pain go away. I cannot stop this priest from forcefully bringing me towards the people; I reach out to grab at something to prevent him, but my hand clutches at thin air. He is preaching, proclaiming that I have come down to minister to the masses, the revered doctor come to pray at the altar of the Santa Maria! And yet, deep within the ecstatic roar of the people, there is a dark undertone, a hostile growl that La Lechusa must be stopped, shouts to grab me and hold onto me and tear me to pieces. Somehow, the gates have been unlocked and I am being pushed forward, into the arms of a wailing mob. There is a sickening crush, the stench of hundreds of decaying bodies pressed against me, trying to grab a lock of my hair, intent on gouging chunks of my skin and slivers of my aura. I have the sensation that I am going under water, that I can't catch my breath. I am drowning.

"Stop! Please stop!" I beg, even as the hands are pulling me deeper into the mob.

"Murderer!" a woman screams, trying to claw her way towards me. "You killed my daughter!"

"Touch me! Heal me!" A man howls, his eyes wild. I saw him shove aside a group of teenage girls in his desperate attempts to get to me. I close my eyes.

"La Lechusa brought the earthquake! She is to blame for all of this!"

Suddenly, the guards appear. There are so many they completely surround me and center me inside a tight wall of security. Somehow, above it all, I can hear Carmen's shouted commands as the guards use heavy sticks to force the mob away from me. There are screams, chants, angry insults. My feet are no longer even touching the ground; I am being carried back through the phalanx of people, across the threshold of the hospital barriers until they release me, cram me back into the dark stairwell. I am shaking so bad I can barely stand – Carmen is there, her strong arms around my waist as she muscles me up the stairs. I can still hear the howling crowds, the clattering of rocks thrown against the door mixed with the praises and Hosannas for Santa Mercedes.

That night, we do not do the rounds. If I had had access to alcohol, I would have drunk myself into bleary semi-consciousness. More people have bypassed the guards and now stand bowing and praying before the hazy image of the Madonna. The water has risen at least an inch since this morning, and most of the city is now wading in at least six inches of brackish salt water. By dawn, there are over one hundred people worshipping at the shrine. By noon, another two hundred have risked climbing the barbed-wire walls and tried to approach the apparition before being beaten off by the guards.

We hear news that a storm is brewing over the ocean, and the waves are starting to crash against the levees. The water rises another inch or two, and the mass of humanity outside of the hospital grows even larger. The storm will bring drinking water to the parched population, prolonging lives that have already become unbearable. Even with the thunder clouds roiling over the city, the image of the Virgin Mary is clearly visible against the backdrop of the black glass. We stand on the fifth floor, and it is hard not to compare our situation to the final days of a lost war, to know that we are witnesses to the end of the world and that nothing will ever be the same again. When it finally arrives, the storm rages for two long days and nights, during which we continue to admit patients and care for the sick. Carmen and I go about our mercenary task of making the rounds, the little silver plate gradually growing lighter and lighter with every pass.

On the third day, the rains stop and a hot, merciless sun emerges to beat down upon the people. We are up to our knees in water now, and it continues to rise. Small children, the feeble, and the old people cannot tolerate the current, and many are being swept away to sea. There are too many bodies to count lying forsaken in the streets; out of necessity, we have become callous to the flesh and blood of another human being. It does not surprise us when news of cannibalism and attacks on defenseless loners become commonplace. In the confines of the wards, the small group of us come together to discuss rations and next steps. Without food, we will be unable to sustain the hospital. We consider making a deal with one of the strongest gangs that has risen out of the collapse of the city; if the gang will hunt and gather food for us, we will supply them with clean water. It seems that every decision we make now is tainted with dealings with the Underworld; what the crowds below lack in nutrition, they have more than made up for with guns and knives.

But instead of getting smaller, the crowds outside the gates have grown in numbers. I wonder what it is that keeps bringing them out from the safety of the mountains and the countryside – don't they understand that by coming below sea level, they will be among the first to perish? The levees grow more fragile, and the people keep coming.

Carmen says that they have come to die with the blessed apparition. She says that the people would rather end their lives in the presence of a deity, instead of dying alone and uncomforted. She believes that the Virgin really is a sign that God is watching over us, and has begun to recite the Hail Mary and the Our Father over the bodies we have administered the poison to. I am not so sure – while I am in awe of the appearance of the figure emblazoned on the black glass, I cannot say that it comforts me. In fact, it does the exact opposite; it fills me with dread.

On the fifth day after the first sighting of Mary, the guards are no longer visible near the entrance barricades. So many people have breached the fences, there is no longer any room on the front lawn of the hospital grounds. In some ways, the thigh-high water is a blessing, as they are unable to move quickly and attempt to attack our building. Due to the rising water, Tent City has disbanded, with the people moving onto the upper floors of any standing structures. Still, we are anxious. We know there are several strong gangs out there with vicious tribal leaders who have risen to the rank of warlord. It is only because we still minister to the sick, still answer the door, and accept the most critical cases that we have not been assaulted yet.

There is a tangible excitement in the air; the priest has announced that there will be a church service at twilight. He will say the Catholic mass, and although there is no bread for communion, he has sanctioned that the people may substitute any consumable food to be used as representation of the Body of Christ. Carmen has indicated that she would like to go down and participate in the mass; I have refused to go with her as I am reluctant to place myself in jeopardy again. I will be alone on the wards this evening for at least a half hour, as most of the staff has decided to attend. In preparation, we move among the writhing patients giving each a few teaspoons of sweetened condensed milk with a little bit of rice mixed in and a ladleful of water which they drink with cracked lips.

In late afternoon, the sound of a bell ringing draws us to the stairwell. The remaining guards are signaling to us that a new casualty has arrived that is worthy of hospital admittance. We run down the stairs with the urgency of our medical training, and cautiously open the sealed doors. What greets us is so unexpected, so horrific in its implications that we are momentarily speechless.

A small group of people in various stages of shock are carried through the doorway, their bodies hammocked on pieces of salvaged tarp. Thin rivers of blood pour out from the corners of the canvasses, ragged chunks of flesh and stumps of arms, what is left of a leg, thighs with roughly torn holes, exposed bone. As they are haphazardly arranged on the cement floor, the people who have carried them to us are all sobbing, talking, wailing in unison. "Tiburón!" we can hear the word, and it makes us go cold. "Sharks! They are coming onto the land!"

Even as I begin assessing the damage, my clinical mind focused on understanding and appraising the extent of injury, I cannot stop the panic surging through my heart. One of the missionaries is attempting to calm everyone, to get the story of what happened. As I listen, my unsterile bare hands delicately probe the lacerated meat of a teenager's knee, the lower half of the leg gone.

"The sharks are swimming in the shallow water, attacking the humans as they stand"... "helpless, in the rising levels of the city streets"... "People are disappearing"... "feeding frenzies"... "red-tinged water sloshing with the waves of the coming fins..."

It is all too much to bear. We transport the patients upstairs, straining under their weight and the burden of the terrible information. As the doctor-in-charge, I give orders to make them as comfortable as possible, cover them with blankets, give instructions in preparation for cauterization. Using fire and some of our larger surgical steel instruments, we will be able to burn the flesh in an attempt to mitigate some of the damage. Carmen stays by my side, knowing that she will be my assistant in the procedures.

A few excruciating hours pass in a blur of seared human flesh, the burnt coagulation of tissues necessary in order to save the life of these starving humans. Three of them never regained consciousness. The remaining two screamed, tied down to the bed, pleading with me to stop, to let them die. *First, do not harm.*

We are exhausted and empty as we leave the side of the last shark victim, our shoulders hunched over, our clothing now covered in a fresh layer of grime. The sound of another hymn reaches our ears, rising from the service that has started below. Thousands of voices are joining together to sing, the sound sweet and uplifting and horribly, absolutely tragic. The staff have begun to leave, to descend the stairs to join the mass. Carmen touches my arm, and I flinch. "I'll be back in a little while," she reassures me before joining the others. The door to the stairwell closes with a sense of finality; I feel the breath of Charon on the back of my neck again. I no longer understand my purpose, my usefulness in this barren new world.

Drawn to the cracked windows, I pull up a battered office chair and sit to watch the Priest minister to the gathered believers. So many people, they stretch out towards the setting sun, hands clutched in worship, ignoring the water as it pools around their legs. I watch, but feel no sense of peace. There is a sensation of pressure in my chest, a lack of ability to take a deep breath. I realize that I am clutching the arms of the chair tightly, my knuckles white. The service is supposed to be uplifting and offer hope to the thousands who have come to participate, but by the slumped shoulders and slack faces of the crowd, it might as well have been a funeral mass.

The water is sloshing around the crowd; it is becoming harder to stay upright. I feel drowsy, and my attention wanders further out to sea.

From my vantage point, I see the tip of an enormous tentacle rise out of the water before anyone else. The alien limb sways in the air for a moment, then reaches gingerly over the brick and rock barriers, as if searching for leverage. I bolt out of my chair. "NO!" I feel as though I am having an out-of-body experience, pounding on the glass and trying to signal to the people below. "LOOK OUT!"

It is massive; a slimy appendage suspended over everything, taller than the 5-story hospital building, lifting up and up and then joined by a second, a third arm, a monster of unimaginable proportions emerging from the darkest layers of the ocean floor. It surfaces slowly, causing great waves to churn and crash as it crawls over the levees and onto the land. It moves like a slug, pulling the weight of its enormous self along the sand, pausing while half in and half out of the water, a hole opening in the side of its gelatinous form, and the dripping jaw of its open mouth as it let out a high pitched screeching sound.

I let out a sob. "No, no, no..." I keep saying as the leviathan begins to crawl towards the mainland, its tentacles poised for attack. Angry and confused by the sudden gravity that is pressuring against its gelatinous body, it lets out another shrill shriek. Horrified, I watch as a second sea creature rises from the depths and answers the original beast with its own monstrous voice. Though burdened by their weight, the two monsters grappled the collapsed buildings and walls, using their massive tentacles to pull themselves across the land. Somehow, they must be following the heat and movement of the crowds, drawn ashore by the scents and stirrings of thousands of unwashed human beings, two prehistoric behemoths dragging themselves towards a meal that has been served to them by the glimmering apparition.

I am helpless. I can only observe, mouth open at the devastation, while the people begin to stampede, to claw one another out of the way of the impassive creatures. The surge of thousands of trapped bodies, the cries, the vision of the tentacles as they seek a body, curl the tip around a squirming, sobbing human before stuffing it into its mouth to be devoured, is surreal. The leviathan is the new god, displacing any memories of Christian, Judaic, Islamic ideals. It opens its maw, greasy and splattered with the viscera of half-chewed flesh, and lets out a bellow that bursts the eardrums of all within its wake. It feeds, unaware of its new place in the world, sloshing its way further inland, delighting in the taste of the mammals, the heat of their body temperatures. The ocean has turned red with spilled blood as the people scatter, most of them heading for higher ground.

I back away from the sight, and stumble backwards into one of the mattresses on the floor. I am struck dumb, unable to speak or cry out, my eyes burning from what I have witnessed. The beasts continue to reach out and grab the poor souls unlucky enough to be within its grasp, their huge teeth gnashing and crunching the bones of the humans as gristle and plasma squirt over the heads of the remaining survivors. There are numerous fins visible in the water now, sharks drawn into the shallow water by the gore and chunks of meat floating around. I can see women, children being knocked off their feet with killing speed, disappearing under the surface in a mist of severed limbs and broken spines. Somehow, I scramble to my feet and begin to run.

The patients, unaware of what is going on outside, begin groaning as soon as they see me; their endless begging for food and water are no different than the sound of the sea monsters. I move quickly around the beds and mattresses, overturning carts and tables as I search. "Where is it where is it where is it?" I am crying, hands flying through cupboards as I seek the treasure, the true salvation. In my delirium, I grab an elderly woman whose left side of her face and all of her nose have been eaten away by a festering wound. "Where is it?" I demand, shaking her.

When no answer is forthcoming, I dash into the next ward and repeat my actions, causing fear and cries for help from the surrounding beds. But it is no use – I don't know where Carmen hides it. I can't find it. The silver dish is nowhere to be found. In my growing madness, I tear across the floor, not caring that I am stepping on hands or feet. I burst into the next hallway and lurch towards the nurse's desks. Amid the peeling ceilings, the mildew, the streaks of mud covering the floors and walls, I continue to search, fingers stretching into the backs of desk drawers, hysterically pulling file cabinets out of the walls. Through it all, I can hear the maddening sounds of destruction, the leviathans continuing to cause chaos as they move across the city streets in anticipation of more prey.

"WHERE IS IT?" I scream, fingernails gouging into the skin of my face. With what must be wild eyes, I stare at the doorway of the tiny bedroom I shared with Carmen. I rush to the room, force the door open and begin tearing apart the sleeping space. I cannot find the silver dish, the precious sugar cubes I must swallow so that I can end all of this madness. I let out a ragged sob, and my eyes fall upon Carmen's pillow. There, underneath the unwashed linens, is the pistol. I cradle it in my hands, caressing the steel. I suddenly get a crazy thought in my head, remembering that my dear friend is out there, defenseless, in the path of the beasts. Without thinking twice, I exit the room and run at full speed towards the stairwell.

Taking the steps two and three at a time, I only get as far as the second floor before I am met with the onrush of people pushing up the stairs, trying to get out of the way of the attacking creatures and the rising ocean. They overwhelm me, and I am forced by the motion of the crowd to turn around, get out of their way by using the second floor exit door to escape being trampled. Out of breath, no longer thinking coherently, I race onto the abandoned floor, holding the pistol to my breasts. A few people have followed me, and then more come piling in through the doorway.

"Santa Mercedes, help me!" a woman cries. Another woman falls prostrate on the floor and begins banging her head in supplication. "Save us!"

"It's her!" a male voice shouts angrily. "La Lechusa! She is the one who has called the beast to do her bidding! She is the reason our families have been murdered!"

"No," I hold up my hand, shaking my head. I back away from them, towards the windows, towards the rainbow-colored apparition that shines at us through the black glass. "Get away from me!"

"You have stayed up here to call upon the monster to destroy us! He is part of your pact with the devil!" Another woman screams, pointing her finger at me. The crowd begins to move towards me, hostile and violent.

"This is your doing, witch! You have caused all of this!" a man picks up a piece of debris and throws it at my head.

"No! I am not the monster!" Turning to stare at the Virgin Mary, I raise the pistol and place the piece in my mouth. "I am not the monster," I whisper, pulling the trigger.

My last awareness is of the image of my brains and gore splattered across the face of the Madonna, blood oozing from the sides of her eyes as if there were tears spilling down her cheeks. The body, my body, crashes through the glass and I am flying, falling above the heads of the desperate crowds.

"Shhh!" a voice, my voice carries with the wind, lifting up my hands, now talons, to the spirits of the dead rising all around me. There is a whistling sound emitting from the hole in my head as the souls turn in the air, following me towards the setting sun.

Clear Water

Kerry G.S. Lipp

Paradise. Well, it should have been but God, or more likely the Devil, shit all over that. It was supposed to be the perfect spring break. It wasn't. There were five of us, and now there are only two. This is what happened.

***

I held my shot high, pointed towards a rare, intimidating, yellow sky, and made a toast.

"To the best spring break ever," I yelled at that sickly sky.

Glasses clinked, and we gulped shots down our throats. I choked it down. I dry heaved. The liquor burned and I couldn't get over the smell of black licorice. Who the hell brings Jagermeister on a boat in 90 degree weather?

Jack, that's who. And he grinned watching me flinch, feigning a vicious gut punch at my solar plexus. There were 5 of us. One couple, Mike and Abby, and three singles, Captain Jack, Krista (the girl I was chasing), and myself.

You can call me Charlie by the way.

I grabbed two beers from the cooler and handed one to Krista.

"I want to show you something," I said, and she followed me to the side of the boat. Captain Jack's father's boat.

"Show me what?" she asked, her perfect white smile stealing my eyes from her beautifully defined, tanned body barely covered by an electric pink bikini. Sweat and oil shimmered on her making her smooth skin look slick.

"Look," I said leaning over, "it's clear water, you can see all the way to the sand at the bottom. I mean it's only a few feet, but have you ever seen water this clear outside of a bottle?"

She laughed at my horrible simile, making me think that she might just be interested. As we were both leaning over, admiring the clear water, the few fish we saw and the white-tan sand underneath, she screamed, dropped her beer over the side, and jumped, spine snapping straight from 90 degrees to 180 degrees in a nanosecond. Startled, I looked at her. Her mouth was open and arms flapped fast as a hummingbird. And then I saw the problem. The top half of her sweet pink bikini was gone and her breasts perked before my eyes. I looked long enough to appreciate the contrast of pale white to tan brown skin before Krista flung her arms across them and turned around. They were titillating.

Behind us stood Captain Jack, lips split in a twisted, victorious smile while he twirled the top like a fluorescent terrible towel. I was too shocked to react, but after a long second I started laughing.

"Asshole," she shouted, reaching to catch it and missing as he pulled it out of reach. He dangled it in front of her, pulled it back, dangled it, pulled it back. Each time she grabbed for it Jack and I were rewarded with another glimpse of her sweet lemon sized breasts.

He wouldn't give it back to her and she finally conceded, wrapping herself inside a beach towel. I couldn't stop laughing. Krista was absolutely pissed, but Jack didn't give in, didn't look guilty, didn't do anything but smile.

And then put them down the front of his swimming trunks. Now he'd probably gone too far, but he was my best friend and twice my size and as I learned real soon, this was not nearly too far.

Captain Jack and I stood next to each other trying not to laugh while Krista sat wrapped in a towel looking like someone just curbed her puppy.

"Hey at least I stuck it in the front," Jack said and farted loud. We all cracked up especially Abby. She was holding her stomach and slopping beer as laughter induced tears gathered and fell from the corners of her eyes.

"I'm sorry," she started, but couldn't finish as another fit of laughter struck her.

Even though she was still raging, and trying to hide it, I glimpsed a flash of hateful laughter on Krista's red face.

"Get fucked Jack," she said coldly, without meeting his eyes.

She looked vulnerable and beautiful and I couldn't look away. She stared at me, pleading with her eyes for me to do something, so I did. I walked toward her, handed her a new beer, put my arm around her.

"I don't know why you're so embarrassed," I said. "You've got a wonderful rack."

"Fuck off," she said, punching me hard in the arm, but I saw a flicker of playfulness under the rage.

Our eyes locked, and even though we'd been engaged in a flirty two month standoff, I caught my first sight of her affection for me. Krista leaned into me and I inhaled deeply, catching the coconut scent of her sunscreen and tilted my head toward the sky, seeing the brooding, but beautiful streaks of ominous pink highlighting the pale yellow.

My friends, as they always seem to have a way of doing, shattered this moment, and while Abby's body rocked with new laughter, Mike snatched her zebra striped top off as well.

"You shit," Abby yelled, giggling. "Fine. I thought these were just for you," she said and stood up. "Apparently Mike wants you all to have a good look, so take it in." She stood in front of us, and all of us, even Krista, took a good look at her breasts, perked like twin exclamation points above her pale stomach.

"Niiiiiiiiiiiiiiiice. Need some more sunscreen?" Jack asked, making no attempt to look away.

We all laughed. Still standing and making no attempt to cover herself, Abby walked toward the cooler and pulled out the bottle of Jager. She tipped the dark brown bottle to her lips and I saw her throat gulp three times, she put the bottle back into the cooler, walked to the middle of the boat, said, "Fuck it," and took her zebra bottoms off too.

I wish I could've seen the expression on Mike's face, but there was no way I was looking away. Even though I was into Krista, Abby was hot as fuck too. I couldn't really see much, other than she was well groomed.

"Alright, now we've got a party," Jack said, stripping off his trunks and throwing them overboard into the water. His dick poked out semi-hard from staring at Abby's naked body.

"Jesus Christ," I said arm still around Krista.

"You dumb fucker," Krista shouted, "My fucking top was in there. Get it, like right now, you dick. This isn't funny anymore."

Mike looked dumbstruck, taking in the naked images of both his girlfriend and Captain Jack. Not to be outdone, Mike stripped off his trunks, threw Abby over his shoulder and jumped into the clear water. The cannonball splash rained on me and Krista, soaking her towel. They surfaced, treading, both heads well above water.

"How deep is it?" I asked.

"I don't know. We can touch. No problem. The sand feels amazing, almost like clay, and the water is warm."

"I can see your little shrimp dork," Jack taunted pointing at Mike's crotch, which was visible through the clear water."

"Shrimp? Shit, it's like a giant squid tentacle."

Laughing, Jack took a five step jog and dove into the water. Like Mike and Abby, his splash landed directly on me and Krista, only the splash didn't seem to end.

Sometime before the splash ended, out of nowhere, the rain began. I looked up and saw something I've never seen before; it was kind of like a sunset, but also not at all like a sunset. It wasn't close to evening. The pink streaks had collected on one half of the sky, and butted right up against that unhealthy yellow. The sky split into two perfect halves, one a brilliant pink, like Krista's floating bikini top. The other that sickly, tobacco-stained-teeth yellow. Like a healing bruise. And from both a warm, almost hot rain was falling. It was surreal and beautiful and the hot tub rain felt wonderful. As I leaned my head forward, I saw Krista looking straight up in awe of the sky as the rain fell. I put one hand on the back of her neck and the other on her chin, pulled her face toward mine and kissed her. With an odd sense of urgency, we kissed passionately under that divided sky with rain falling like hot shower water all over us.

She ended the kiss with a devilish smile. She stood, dropping her towel and started walking with definite purpose across the boat.

"That's the spirit, take it all in," Jack said, staring.

"Oh it's all going in," she answered, throwing Jack's towel overboard. Then she crossed to the other side of the boat and chucked one of his shoes out to sea. She did the same with his other shoe and his t-shirt. Jack's stuff was scattered like diving sticks in all directions from the boat.

"Come on you crazy bitch," he protested. Everyone was laughing, except Jack.

"Bitch? You never should have said that," she answered grabbing his phone.

"NO! Don't you fucking dare!" he yelled, sprint-swimming toward the boat.

Krista cocked her arm back holding the phone like a tiny baseball. Flinging her arm forward, she grinned at him.

"Fun isn't it?" She brought her arm down without releasing Jack's phone.

"Thank you," he said, out of breath and grateful.

Then the thunder hit.

It roared unlike any thunder I'd ever heard. It started with a low rumble, like bowling pins knocked for a strike or a drum roll played on a bass drum, slowly rising in pitch and climaxing, shrieking like a banshee in an acid bath. It lasted a long time.

Then the lightning hit, also unlike any bolt any of us had ever seen. None of us missed it because it lit up the sky for a solid ten seconds. Its jagged shape shot down from the exact point where the two shades of sky converged. The lightning struck the deserted beach a few hundred yards away, looking both static and tangible as it connected the sands to the heavens while we all gaped.

And when the massive bolt finally fizzled out, I saw the first of many things that will ruin sleep for the rest of my life.

"Get back to the fucking boat!" I screamed, but none of them moved. They were awestruck. At the point where the flash hit, the sand was turning a bright, bloody crimson. It spread in all directions, slowly turning all of the sand rage-red.

I could see the color spreading through the clear water, like a red tide of sand flowing directly underneath the surf. It crept closer and closer until it went directly underneath Mike, Jack, Abby and the boat. Horrified and screaming, Krista rushed over to me.

"What the…" was all she could get out.

The hot rain continued to fall, but I felt nothing but the cold sweat dripping down my whole body. The three of them struggled in the clear water, now with a reddish backdrop.

"Get to the boat now," I said.

Then, at the same time, all three of them said the same thing that froze my spine despite the fervent rain.

"My feet are stuck."

"What do you mean?" I asked looking over the boat rails. And then I saw it. All six of their feet were buried ankle deep in that bloody red sand.

"Can you swim? Can you tread? Pull your feet out! We gotta get outta here."

"I can't," Jack shouted, "can you guys?"

"No. I'm stuck. I'm fucking scared," Mike said starting to unravel.

Abby's face turned ghost white and she said nothing. She just trembled, making small whimpers, her lips quivering. She sniffled, tried to hide it.

"Abby, answer us, are you ok?"

Her whimpers became shrieks of pain and finally her muffled words became clear and terrifyingly loud. All she

34

said, over and over, her mantra loud enough to rip vocal cords was, "IT HURTS. IT HURTS. IT HURTS."

Jesus.

I tried to say calm.

"Mike, Jack are you guys in pain?"

"No, I'm stuck but no pain," Mike said.

"Same," said Jack.

Then I felt Krista's grip on my arm. She had lost all color, she couldn't make a sound, could barely breath, but she raised her hand and pointed towards Abby's legs.

"IT HURTS. IT HURTS."

Under the clear water I could see at least a dozen jellyfish throwing themselves into her legs. Some stuck, some hit, swam back and then hit again. Wrapped their tentacles tight and pulsed their gooey bodies while they attacked.

"IT HURTS."

They were all over her. I could no longer see her legs, they were just a mass of amorphous convulsing gray. My blood froze in my veins when I remembered she had gone in naked. I shuddered. So had the guys. More were swimming her way and soon her entire submerged body was coated in jellyfish like a body cast made of soft, stinging filth. She passed out, legs still stuck in the sand, but hinged at the hip, neck bent with her face submerged in the water. I leapt to the stern of the boat, ready to go after her when Krista jerked me back by the waistband of my trunks.

"No! You'll get stuck too!"

She was probably right. Abby's head popped up, snapped back, eyes as big and white as golf balls rolling back in her head while she screamed, "IT HURTS."

I got ready to jump again. Krista stopped me.

"We can't just watch them die," I yelled and shoved her away.

"You can't leave me alone," she screamed back.

"Fine, but we've gotta do something."

"Yes," she said, took a breath and she was calm.

We looked back at the water. Some of the jellyfish were leaving Abby, heading towards Jack who saw them coming, but it was Mike who screamed next. The only way I can describe the scream is that it was the scream of a man whose balls were being ripped apart by crabs. Big crabs. It was hard to tell through the rippling water, but their legs looked at least 6 inches long. And their numbers were legion.

Unlike Abby, Mike fought back. He pulled a crab out of the water, its body alone the size of his head. Its spidery legs kicked in the air as it tried to scuttle and free itself.

Mike started ripping.

"Krista, pull the anchor, Charlie, start throwing stuff, maybe we can scare them away," Jack commanded. His orders broke our trance and we got busy.

Before I turned away I saw Mike, every muscle straining, dismember a crab, throw the pieces as far as he could, let out a war cry and grab another one, but they were all over him. The clear water slowly started to swirl with fresh spilled blood from cuts made by their jagged pinchers. It started to turn pink, like saliva after flossing. Through that sick, clear pink I saw more jellyfish and a lone sting ray fast approaching.

"HELP ME. COME ON YOU FUCKERS!" Jack screamed, fresh pain in his voice. I couldn't see him and I didn't want to guess what was now attacking him.

I grabbed the cooler and slid it to the edge, trying to figure out who needed help the most. Through the pounding rain, I started throwing beers at the jellyfish covering Abby. The water slowed the full cans down, making them harder to aim, and even though a couple connected, they just bounced off the cellulite bodies.

"The fucking anchor's stuck in the sand," Krista cried.

Mike ripped another crab apart and I threw a few beers towards his midsection. None of the crabs scattered. Pieces of the dead ones floated in a spiky circle around Mike. Some of their severed legs still twitched.

"Cut it! Knife is under the captain's seat," Jack yelled, voice cracking in pain. "Oh fuck. God."

About 20 snaky fish had attached their mouths all over his lower body. It looked like his body had tentacles. I later learned that these were a parasitic eel called a lamprey, known for attaching themselves to fish and feeding by slowly sucking out the insides of their prey. Some blood seeped through their sucking mouths, staining the clear water pink, then red.

"Charlie, tie two of the ropes to the stern and throw them out to me," Jack commanded, somehow coherent despite what was going on below the surface of the water. He was getting his fucking guts sucked out.

As I started tying the ropes, I saw Mike's eyes begin to glaze over as he kept ripping crabs, but they never stopped coming. I could see more and more marching across the red sand. A quick glance at Abby showed her once again face down, passed out, drowning in the pinky clear water. I had no idea how long she had been like that.

Krista saw Abby's face submerged and screamed at her. Abby didn't flinch. Krista bit her lip, and with tears running down her cheeks lobbed a full beer. She tossed the bottle (we'd thrown all the cans) at Abby's head. It struck her and her head popped up. The bottle split her skin, leaving a fresh cut in the top of her head and spilling blood down her face. She gasped, disoriented, not knowing where she was or what was going on. And then she started screaming again.

I thought it might've been more merciful to just let her drown.

Krista went back to sawing the anchor.

"Anchor's cut," she said, sounding scared. "What now?"

"We're gonna pull 'em out. Get ready to drive and when I say hit the throttle, hammer it!"

I threw the ropes out to Jack, his body even more covered in lampreys. The sting ray had gone for back up and now six giant rays surrounded my three friends. Not attacking, just circling, watching, taunting. Haunting. The fear I felt watching a school of sting rays gracefully gliding towards my defenseless best friends was bottomless.

And I could see it all through that sickly pink, clear water. The rippling tide continued to shift. Shapes and colors of the attacking fish underneath turned it into a brilliantly disturbing artwork. And those shapes preyed on my friends and my friends screamed.

Jack grabbed the ropes and wound each around his arms as many times as he could, making two thin, taught cords between him and the boat.

"Now!" he shrieked, voice wary, agonized.

"Gun it Krista, hard as it'll go!"

She thrust the throttle and the boat jerked to life. It jolted fast, cutting briefly through a few feet of water before halting. Jack's face read ungodly strain. Cords in his neck bulged to burst, but he uttered no cry, his face pure determination.

"Harder Krista, push it harder!"

"I am," she said racking the throttle as hard as she could. "It's like we're still anchored." The boat groaned, fighting the stalemate. I grabbed one of the ropes with both hands and jerked like a game of tug of war.

Nothing.

"Krista, back it off and try again."

Their screams shredded my eardrums. Ropes loosening, rain pounding, water pink, sky split, I grabbed a rope and she gunned it again. It seemed like the boat moved a little further and we were going to pull him out.

Until I saw Jack's arms tear free in a spray of blood and stringy tissue.

"Stop," I screamed, but it was too late. Both of Jack's arms came apart at the shoulder sockets with a splitting pop I heard over the boat engine and the screaming. His face contorted to that of a demon suffering eternally in the fires of hell as he looked down at the remnants of his arms. Squirts of blood turned the clear water a cloudier shade of the sand gripping his feet. The ropes shot back to the boat, both arms landing on the deck, still bleeding, still twitching.

"No. NO!" my voice raw to the point that I actually spit blood. I put my head in my hands as their shrieks pierced my ears like splinters under toenails. All of my hope ran out the corners of my eyes and down my face. Krista came to me, looked out at the water, saw the mayhem beneath it tinged pink and turning red fast, heard the screams and whimpers of our dying friends and bowed her forehead to touch mine.

"What happens now?" she asked. It took her a few seconds to get these words out.

Then the boat started rocking.

"That much blood in the water? Probably sharks," I said, oddly calm. At this point all of my friends were in shock. Abby's face was down in the water again for God knew how long, Jack was bleeding out faster than the rain was coming down, and Mike was whimpering above water, exhausted, arms futilely smacking the spiky, hard shells of crabs below.

The boat rocked hard again and I looked over the side. Have you ever seen a shark up close? With no aquarium glass dividing you? Gray skin, feral eyes and teeth like a bear trap. Boat swaying, threatening to capsize I broke the stare with the shark as it darted toward the blood-spewing stumps of Jack's ruined arms. The shark hit him at full speed, a car with teeth, cutting him in half. The top half went with the shark, lower half stayed, embedded firmly in the crimson sand. It was impossible to tell if the sand still colored the water, or if it was just the blood of my friends. Several other fins cut fast through the water in all directions. Abby and Mike were next, and there was nothing we could do.

Too weak and shocked to scream I simply turned toward Krista with my hopeless hands hanging. Her hands held an oar. The last thing I remember is her winding up like an old pro and the split second explosion of pain I felt before crumpling to the floor, out cold.

***

I woke up in a hospital room, heart monitor beeping, IV in my arm, local news on the television above my bed.

Where am I?

I tried to remember, but I couldn't. The news cut to the latest headlines and that shot me straight up like someone had shocked my chest with a defibrillator. There was no sound, but I could see the pictures of my friends. Rage and sadness warred in my head, ending in a draw as I simultaneously started crying and screaming for a nurse.

One came rushing with Krista at her back. My head ached.

"What the hell is going on?" I asked.

"You've suffered a pretty severe concussion, and all things considered, you're lucky to be alive. We need to keep you under watch, make sure you don't go comatose. Is there anything I can get for you?"

"My head feels like a battlefield. Can you give me something?"

"Would it be ok if you gave us a minute please?" Krista asked the nurse.

"Yes, but only a minute while I get some medicine. Charlie needs to rest."

When we were alone Krista laughed, but it was not a good laugh, it was defeated, hopeless, horrified.

"I'm sorry," she said.

"For?"

"Putting you here. I whacked you pretty good with that oar."

I felt more confused than angry and the memory came back to me.

"Yeah what was that about?"

"Charlie," the tears started spilling, but her voice didn't waver, "My survival instinct took over. Sharks were butting our boat, and our friends were being eaten alive. We watched Jack lose his arms and then get torn apart by a shark. I couldn't stay there and watch the other two die. I just couldn't. I knew you'd fight, never give up and help them no matter what the cost. That's the kind of person you are, but it was hopeless. Maybe cowardly, maybe not but there was nothing else we could do."

"You're probably right," I sighed, "I couldn't stand those screams, seeing those creatures torture our friends. What did we do wrong?"

"Nothing, we did everything right. We just couldn't win."

"But we left. You knocked me out and we left them behind."

"Charlie please…"

"No I could've stopped the oar. I could've gone into the water with the knife and avoided the sand. I know what I could've done. I could've cut their feet off, pulled them out, saved them."

"Charlie, stop. You saw what happened when the blood hit the water, cutting them would have just brought that sooner. And if you would've touched that sand…" she trailed off.

"You don't know that," I said. "We left them behind."

"Charlie," she took my hand, leaned over to kiss my cheek, spilling clear tears on my gown, "I made the decision so you didn't have to. I did it. I knocked you out. YOU HEAR ME. I FUCKING DID IT! You should have no guilt, I saved you from that. I have to live with that. I did it to protect you so please, I'm begging you, listen to me, you have nothing to feel guilty about."

"Yeah," I said refusing to meet her eyes.

"I guess that's a start," she said and kissed my forehead. "Get some rest, we'll talk more later." Her hand lingered on mine for a moment, a tear falling from each of her eyes. She sniffled. Then Krista turned and lingered for a moment before she slowly walked away.

The nurse returned, giving me a mild painkiller and a cup of clear water. "You've been through a lot," she said, "but you're going to be okay, just get some rest."

"Yeah," I said absently.

I put the pills in my mouth and held the cup up, studying the water. I pondered what scared me more: dark water or clear water. Fear of the unknown or being able to watch everything you fear as it devours everything you love.

Through the clear cup and the clear water I saw Krista's back as she walked out. She was wearing a red shirt and that sick color swam through the water and into my eyes and I knew then that clear water would haunt me for the rest of my life. I sighed and drank in that which would always haunt me and that which I would need to drink in everyday just to survive.

Krista's words fogged in my head as the pain killer kicked in and my eyes started getting lazy. I drifted into a tranquil land of clear water tinged with blood and red sand. A pseudo-paradise of bisected yellow and pink sky, hungry sea creatures and never ending screams. Alone, with nothing to help me stop the screaming.

And unless I gouged my eyes out, I'd always be able to see it all.

I considered the idea and it sounded better and better as I recovered.

I'd made my decision.

I'd rather fear the unknown than watch it all happen.

Chlorine

Blaise Torrance

"This is nearly as good as an abandoned theme park," Willow said with relish, raising her digital camera to snap more photos of the water park's dark glass front, "or an old *mental hospital*. How long since it was closed down?"

"Ten years." Kate had been twelve years old the last time she had been standing here with her swim bag in hand, and the water park had closed soon after that last visit.

"Do you think there will be a way in?" Willow lowered her camera, suddenly suspicious. "What about security guards?"

"There's nothing to steal," Kate said. She set her bag down and knelt to rummage through the contents. The last time she had come to the water park, she had packed a towel, anti-chlorine shampoo and her first bikini. The bikini had been blue, she remembered, and she'd been afraid to go on the water slides while wearing it because the top rode up easily on her flat chest.

Today, she had brought a torch, a spare set of batteries and half a broken house brick. She hefted the brick thoughtfully in one hand, taking up a good grip. The murky glass was already cracked at eye-level and it shattered at the first blow. The trapped air inside smelled hot and unclean like a cloudy fish tank left standing in the sun.

Willow made a fluttery sound of panic, plump hands flying to her black-painted mouth as Kate began to methodically hammer away at the broken glass, knocking out long shards until the frame was empty. No alarms began to wail and when Kate stepped inside, Willow followed after a moment of indecision, as Kate had known she would. Willow fancied herself a photographer and had developed a fascination with creepy abandoned buildings, even though her only previous bit of urban exploration had been cut short after she had broken into a closed school and been chased straight back out by an angry tramp.

Willow began to take her photos. Kate flicked her torch on and played the beam around the reception area, remembering the string of girls who had once sat at that desk. They had worn skimpy tops that left their tanned arms bare even in winter, their hair billowing gently in the steamy air and make-up bleeding into hot, damp skin. Most of the staff had been local teenagers, and Kate had wanted to get a summer job here too once she was old enough. It had seemed vaguely exotic to her, almost like working on a tropical beach somewhere far away.

But then the park had closed. Kate let her torch skip over the desk where those pretty girls had once sat. There was a pile of leaflets left on the desk advertising yearly family passes to the water park, the inks bleached to weak blues and greys. Next to that, there was a stack of free activity sheets for children to take with them and fill out during their visit.

There was a hand print in the dust that had gathered on the activity sheets, small and delicate as if a child had pressed their hand there just minutes before.

"Kate?"

Willow had stopped taking photos of the mural on the opposite wall, a faded painting of the water park's cartoon mascots Sharky McBill and Petey Pirate digging up treasure on a tropical island.

"Do you know why this place closed?"

"Health and safety," Kate said, pressing her own hand to the activity sheet and leaving an adult-size print that obliterated the small mark. "The lifeguards weren't trained and there were accidents. And then some kids went missing."

"Missing?" Willow's voice rose, suitably impressed by how creepy that was. "You're not joking?"

"Three of them," Kate said. She picked up the activity sheet and gently shook away the years of dust. Someone had marked off most of the scavenger hunt list with big childish ticks, but there was one more item left to find. "Come on. Let's go take your photos."

Willow followed in awed silence. There had always been a chaotic background of noise in the park, amplified by all those hard surfaces. Screams of laughter, the smack of bare feet from children ignoring the 'No Running' signs, the constant suck and wash of water in the chutes and flumes. Now there was only their hollow footsteps to break the silence, and the sounds shivered and died in the thick hush that had fallen over the park.

Kate turned towards the women's changing rooms. She

thought that she could have switched her torch off and still walked there unerringly in the darkness, known exactly when to reach out for the hand rails so she didn't slip on the four tiled steps leading down into the changing rooms. Though of course, the steps wouldn't be wet and slippery now. The pools had been dry for the last ten years.

The familiar smell of warm chlorine and damp towels still permeated the changing rooms. Kate had always liked the smell of chlorine, though when she got older she had begun to complain about how it clung to her skin and gave her blonde hair a greenish tinge, and she had come to the water park less often. Sadie had been unhappy about that. She would have come to the park every day if she could.

"This is amazing," Willow was saying, her voice fading as she wandered away. Bursts of staticky-white camera flashes punctuated the darkness. "I can't believe there's no graffiti anywhere."

Kate played the torch over the mirrors mounted along one wall. Her reflection looked unfamiliar some days, this sensible young woman's face with her light make-up and highlighted hair worn in a short, professional style. She closed her eyes, a little dizzy, as if the room was expanding around her or as if she was *shrinking*, her dense adult flesh sloughing away like a cocoon. With her eyes shut, she could almost feel the weight of her damp ponytail resting between her shoulder blades, the tightness of fresh scabs at her elbows and knees, the deep ache in her teeth as braces inexorably reshaped her gappy, crooked child's smile into an adult's broad and perfect grin.

She opened her eyes and there was a flash of movement behind her in the mirror as something darted through the darkened room. The quick slap of bare feet rang across the shower floor. Kate whirled around and dropped the torch, the light instantly going out.

"What? What is it? Did you hear someone?" Willow sounded scared. Kate ignored her and dropped to her knees, sweeping her hands across the scummy floor until she found the torch.

She stood up, flicking the light back on. "Sadie?"

The shower curtains had dried in stiff creases and she could not see if there was anyone behind them. Kate let the light play over the floor, the white tiles webbed with dark green scum, and knew that she was right. They had not found the body at the park, but Sadie was tethered here. Her long dark hair was caught up in the black plugs that choked the shower drains. The three sets of Kate's goggles she had borrowed and then lost in quick succession would still be down the back of the lockers, dusty and forgotten. One of the yellow certificates thickly papering the walls upstairs would still bear her name from the Pirates and Plunder activity day she had taken part in during her last summer, the oldest girl in the group.

And her laughter might still echo back and forward between the tiled walls, the sound grown so weak and faint that only Kate could hear it.

Kate pulled back the curtains. Sadie was not there.

***

Willow was angry with Kate for scaring her, and kept threatening to go home as she followed Kate out of the changing rooms and up to the water park's coffee bar.

49

"Maybe you should," Kate agreed softly. She discreetly scrubbed her hand on her jeans, wiping away the tangled dark hair clotted between her fingers. It was still damp. "I don't think it's safe here."

"Why not?" Willow turned to her, the camera held up in her hands like a squirrel with an acorn. Despite her threats, she had resumed taking photos of the stairs leading from the swimming pools up to the jungle-themed coffee bar, snapping the fake foliage and the stuffed tropical animals decorating the bannisters, all furred thickly with years of dust.

"Did you ever hear voices coming from the pipes when you were a child?"

"Yeah?" Willow looked confused. "I think most kids do. I didn't brush my teeth for three weeks once because I thought I could hear something saying my name in the U-bend. Why?"

Because a week ago, I was lying in the bath and I could hear sounds underwater, Kate wanted to say. *Like small hands knocking against the side of the bath, the kind of sounds I hadn't heard since I was a little girl. Then I heard them whispering my name in the pipes.*

"I was just wondering," Kate said, and leaned over the balcony. "It seems like a lot of children hear those voices."

She rested her arms on the fake timber and hessian rope, looking down into the dry indoor pools. She used to sit up here with Sadie, perched on the coffee bar stools trying to look sophisticated and hoping the boys from school would come over to talk to her. If they'd ever come, it would have been for Sadie, who was already filling out her own first bikini. Sadie could have passed for fifteen, Kate's mother used to say, with her long legs and developing chest and tilted hazel eyes.

Kate's mother had said a lot of things about Sadie. Her family was *rough,* she would put it delicately, meaning the tattooed father rumoured to have spent time in prison and the mother down at the pub every night, her lips painted a glossy fuchsia and her tanned breasts spilling out of her tight lycra tops. She had pursed her lips when Kate had asked for admission money for two because Sadie never had any money of her own, and when she found out that Sadie borrowed Kate's towel to dry off, she had theatrically made a point of running it through a boil wash by itself every time Kate went swimming.

"You can pick things up from towels," she had said darkly, but never clarified what. There had just been that hint that girls like Sadie were *dirty*, that they didn't come to water parks to swim, that they came here in their bikinis for something else altogether.

She was wrong. Sadie hadn't been the precocious little hussy that Kate's mother had imagined, she hadn't wanted to grow up at all. And she had come to the park purely because she loved water. The languid soaks in the bubbling spa pool, the cold bite of the water as they leapt together hand-in-hand from the outdoor diving boards, the stinging slap of the wave pool, Sadie had loved it all.

And the Hydra, of course. Kate looked up to where the Hydra's enclosed chute entered the main building with a sharp turn that had always thrown Kate and Sadie up the inside wall as though they were weightless. The pastel blue chute was mottled with dirt and rusty orange streaks ran from the metal fixtures like tears. It was still suspended from the ceiling, but she could see where the bolts had worked loose.

"How much would they have to pay you to ride that now?" Willow asked, all her fear gone as she gleefully snapped more photos of the decaying water chute.

"They couldn't pay me enough," Kate said. "Look at the drop." The chute was nearly forty feet above the tiled floor, and higher still outside where the ride started in a separate glass tower. She doubted it could take an adult's weight after ten years of neglect.

"Maybe that was one of the accidents," Willow suggested. "Part of the chute collapsing. I heard about an accident like that. Some college students were trying to set a record for the most people to ride on a water chute at once and it couldn't take their weight."

Kate shook her head. "A couple of people got their hair caught in the pool filters," she said. "Someone fell from the diving board, hit their head and drowned, that sort of thing."

"Kids?"

"No. Never the children." The brittle words seemed to fall from Kate's mouth, shattering in the dry, dusty air. Only adults had died at the water park. Children had just disappeared.

She looked at Willow, short and chunky in her black dress and combat boots, her hair cut in a bob and dyed the glossy black of a Halloween wig. The dirty fish-bowl light seemed to leech the colour from her skin, giving her round face the unhealthy solid whiteness of drowned flesh. In between the soft clicks and whirrs of the camera, Kate could hear a whisper that may have only been the trees outside.

"I think you should probably go now," she said.

Willow goggled at her. "What? Just me?"

"Just you," Kate agreed. "I don't think it's safe here. Not for adults."

Willow gave a sharp bark of surprised laughter. "What do you mean? And you're *twenty two*. You're older than I am!"

Yes, Kate would have said, *but the pipes have begun to talk to me again, and I can hear her voice among them. I think it might be okay. I think I should have stayed with her that first time, but I don't think it's too late for me now.*

"My friend was one of the missing children," she said instead, drawing abstract patterns on the dusty balcony with her forefinger. "Her name was Sadie. She was the last one to disappear, before they closed the water park for good. She went on Hydra." Kate pointed at the chute high above their heads. "She wanted me to come with her, but I stayed here. It was the only time she ever went on the chute alone, and she never came back."

One at a time, the sign had said, but none of the attendants had objected too much if Kate and Sadie climbed in at the same time. It was more fun like that. Sometimes they'd squeeze in together and slide down holding hands, face to face, their screams bouncing off the chute's curved walls as the slipped and slid and fell on top of each other, bruising each other with sharp elbows and knees. Sometimes Sadie would climb in first and Kate behind her, her arms wrapped about her friend's waist as they slid down together, muffling her screams in Sadie's damp, tangled hair.

The best bit was at the very end. The chute went into a steep drop in nearly complete darkness, shooting faster and faster until they burst back out into the light, water drops sparkling and shattering around them as they fell into the splash pool below. Kate had always been a little scared by the splash pool and that moment when she plunged straight to the bottom, toes grazing against the tiled floor, her nose burning with warm salty water, unable to tell which way was up. But Sadie was always there, her slim, strong hand pulling Kate up from the churning water, the two of them wading triumphantly out together.

"It was that stupid bikini," Kate said. "It always used to ride up on chutes and slides. And there were some teenagers from secondary school sat in the coffee bar. I wanted to be like them. I thought water slides were for kids."

She rubbed at her eyes. They were beginning to sting painfully, but not with tears. It was chlorine, seeping out from the long dry, pastel-blue walls of the swimming pools.

"Did someone take them?" Willow was agog. "Were they abducted?"

"Like some kind of sex offender?" Kate had believed it until recently. "That's what the newspapers thought."

"I am *so* sorry." Willow gave Kate a clumsy hug, and her hair smelled damp and salty when it should smell like hair dye and cherry shampoo. "I had no idea. Is that why you don't think it's safe here?"

"Yes." Kate's breath hitched. "Could you wait out the front for me? I need a minute."

She sat down on one of the stools. Her eyes were burning raw and red as if she had just been swimming without her goggles. Kate had believed it was an abduction for years.

A *bad man*, her mother had delicately put it as if Kate had been six years old, someone who had come here by himself and watched the children and patiently lured three of them away over the years. No bodies had ever been found.

A few minutes passed before Kate heard the soft insectile clicks and whirrs of the camera coming from somewhere below the balcony. Willow hadn't left after all. She stood up and leaned over the balcony, but she couldn't see Willow's glossy dark head moving among the dry pools.

"Willow?" she called out, but no one answered. The camera had fallen silent too.

Kate went down the steps to the main pools, her hand trailing lightly through the dusty plastic foliage. The kiddie pool was beneath the balcony and she stepped down into it, imagining the warm slap of water about her knees. The pool was dry, but the footsteps leading to the orange octopus slide at the centre were wet, and they were very small.

She found the camera lying half way across the pool. The last picture was frozen on screen, taken after the camera had been dropped. Two bare feet stood in front of the lens, like a child's, but not quite right. Kate tried to find the zoom function to look closer, and the screen went black. A thin trickle of rusty water ran out of the sides and spattered emptily at her feet.

"Willow?"

A soft, strangled whisper, gurgling up from a throat full of water.

Kate followed the wet footsteps to the plastic octopus in the centre of the pool. Each leg was a slide, no higher than seven feet and high-walled so that no child could fall out as they slid down into the shallow pool. Olly Octopus had done his job well. Kate couldn't remember a single child hurting themselves on those slides.

She had to stoop underneath the hollow body to reach the ladder where the children had climbed up inside. There were the prints of fingers on the dusty rungs, and the ladder creaked alarmingly as she put one foot on it, just enough to boost her head and shoulders inside the octopus's round body.

Sadie was not in the octopus. Willow was there, curled up to fit in a space too small for an adult. Water ran from her open mouth and her black hair leaked dye, a grey puddle collecting in the orange plastic beneath her head. Fingerprint bruises were stamped into her white forearms, smaller than even Sadie's and Kate's fingers had been back then.

Kate pressed two fingers to Willow's throat. No pulse. She should have told Willow the whole story, Willow had readily believed in ghosts and ESP and aliens, and she had been easily spooked. She would have changed her mind and stayed away from the water park, even if Kate couldn't explain exactly what she feared. *I think something lives in the water. I think it always has, and that's why our ancestors threw swords and shields into lakes and springs, why they cut their prisoners' throats and shattered their skulls and gave their bodies to the bog.*

And whatever it was, Kate thought it was still here, even though people thought they had tamed water. They could collect it and pump it full of disinfectant, pipe it into their homes at the twist of a tap and measure it into shallow pools for children to play with, but this clear, blue-tinged water was no safer than a murky loch full of drifting bones and bronze offerings. If sacrifices were not freely given, it would take its own tithe.

A child's high, clear laughter rang out behind her. Kate scrambled to look out through the cloudy plastic portals, seeing the water park as the children had once seen it from their small, secret view, but she could not see Sadie.

Sadie wasn't in the empty spa pool either where they had once lounged in comfortable, drowsy silence, stupefied by the heat. She wasn't in the wave pool where they had held hands as rock music began to pound and the wave machine powered up, holding each other above the water's surface, dragging each other down.

A hollow knock came from above, the sound of a hand bumping against a plastic wall. Kate glanced up at the chute, and knew where Sadie would be.

***

The chute entrance was inside a tower near the outdoor pools. The tower had once been so bright it had hurt to look at it in the sun, nearly four stories of sparkling glass and steel. The entrance was fashioned to look like a sea serpent's gaping mouth, the fierce scarlets and emeralds now faded to weak pastels. Kate remembered the countless times she had seen Sadie disappear ahead of her between those blunt fibreglass teeth.

She wondered if Sadie had ran this way by herself at the end, running because she was eager to ride the chute, not because it had been cold outside on that summer's day. Or maybe she had trudged up the stairs slowly, somehow aware that it would be the last time and that Kate would not stay with her.

But Kate was so much older now. Adults didn't disappear in the water park, they only died.

She closed her eyes and listened to the sigh of the wind shredding itself on the broken glass, listening until she heard the echo of bare feet on the steps and a thin ribbon of long ago laughter.

When she opened her eyes again, she was three-quarters of the way up the tower and out of breath as if she had run. The floor seemed to quiver unsteadily beneath her weight and Kate continued up the stairs more cautiously. Most of the glass was missing near the top and there were holes in the roof, three buckets filled with stagnant water beneath the worst of it.

Kate peered into the mouth of the chute, and the tunnel had never looked so dark, even though she could now see chinks of light where the plastic segments had warped and pulled apart. She picked up the buckets one after another and poured the water down the chute's throat until the thick dust darkened and ran in a sludgy black stream, and the plastic was slick enough to slide down.

Kate climbed into the chute mouth and sat there with her eyes closed. The tower creaked and groaned in the wind and she could hear the distant spatter of water hitting the concrete sixty feet below, but if she listened hard enough, she could imagine the cheers and jeers of children queuing behind her eager for their turn. Kate waited until she could feel the billow of warm air blowing up from the splash pool and hear the other voices, the whispers from the pipes, the wet gurgle of laughter, and beneath it all was Sadie.

Fingers prised insistently at her own, pulling them away from the edge of the chute. Those little fingers were terribly sharp but they were nearly like a child's, so long as she didn't look. Kate kept her eyes tight shut though they streamed with tears, painting wet stripes down her cheeks and running into the corner of her mouth. She licked her lips and tasted chlorine.

As her fingers came loose one by one and she began to slip into the chute's open mouth, Kate wondered if the whispering voices would still take her. She wondered what would happen if they didn't.

Payment

Brent Abell

Now

A chill ran down Danny King's spine and chased the last bit of warmth from the scotch away. His head pounded from the booze and the breeze blowing across the bay reminded him of his trips to the island with his father and grandfather when he was a boy. He had little idea the water and the island they traveled to so many years ago would be his destiny years later.

The island, the water, oh how I wish I could take it all back, he thought and took another long pull from the bottle. The burn ignited his insides and he took a drag from the cigarette hanging from his lips.

Behind him on the rocky hill, the beams from the lighthouse cut through the approaching fog. The horn called out its nightly wail to those in the bay bringing their fishing boats in from another day. When the lights struck the rolling fog they vanished, devoured by the oncoming murkiness. Danny could make out the ships racing back to the docks disappear as the mysterious vapor caught them from behind. In his head he swore he heard their dying screams and the guilt of everything happening around him weighed more heavily on his soul.

The last drop of alcohol ran from the bottle into Danny's mouth and he chucked the empty container over the ledge. He heard the glass shatter on the rocks below as well as the waves hitting the shore, pulling the shards out into the bay. He snorted and stifled back a laugh, his life broken like the bottle and now the end quickly seemed to be bearing down on him.

The island; the place haunted his dreams and consumed his life for the last ten years. It took his family, his career, and his life. He didn't blame Nancy for leaving him a few years ago. He'd become a crazed alcoholic nutcase. She'd finally had enough the night he held her by the throat and babbled on about the spirits of the past and how he was their gatekeeper. Now the island threatened to take the town he held dear. White Creek sat in the path of the cloud coming to claim him, to make him pay what was owed.

***

Ten Years Earlier

"This is the last time we're bringing you out here Danny," his father said patting him on the back.

"We think you're ready to take your place in the family line," Danny's grandfather exclaimed proudly and lit another cigarette.

They led him through the trees until they came across

an ancient stone wall. Within the crumbling stone were three cracked and moss covered tombstones. A small opening in the wall was the only entrance into the cemetery.

"What's this?" Danny asked and squinted to read the dates etched on the old markers.

"These are our forefathers. They helped to found White Creek and we are in their debt. Our family has been tasked in making sure the stones stay unbroken," his father answered.

"The markers?"

"No, the walls. Should they be broken, it is the guardian's role to pay," his grandfather said and turned away.

"Our time is finished, we've guarded this sacred land for two generations and we're tired," his father stated and hugged him.

"What do you mean?" Danny questioned.

His grandfather came up and placed his hands on his shoulders. For a moment, their gazes locked and he saw something in the old man's eyes he'd never seen before: fear. The moonlight cutting through the treetops illuminated his face and the lines etched across his cheeks and forehead were more pronounced.

"Danny, since the town's beginning, folks have been tasked with doing things they never thought they'd have to do. Our family is one of the five guardian clans in the town. Each family has to protect the resting places of our ancestors to keep what they did contained," his father explained.

"What did they do?"

"They had to protect themselves and ensure the town's

survival above everything else. These markers are just for show. Out there, in the water is where their bodies rest," his father explained.

"Then why do they have the stones here Dad?"

"Three men left the town to search for help the first winter after the original founders arrived. Once they were clear of the shore, a dense fog rolled in and they were never seen again. A diary left by one their widows, spoke of the screams they heard within the fog and how it retreated to the island once the unholy cries ceased."

"The fog came here?"

"Yes son, it came back to this spot. From what was handed down, when Josiah White and the expedition came to find out what happened here, they found the town abandoned. Nothing looked disturbed, but they found water all over the houses and shelters. They didn't find another soul. They did find the diaries of a few settlers and it led them here. What happened next, nobody is sure of. Whatever is here is bound by the markers of the three who departed and the wall around them. All we know is that our sacred duty is to safeguard the wall and the markers. If they were to break or fall, the consequences would be dire indeed," his father said and took one last drag from the cigarette he'd been slowly puffing on.

"It is time Danny," his grandfather said.

Grandfather, father, and son all looked to one another. Danny backed away and stepped toward the entryway into the cemetery. His father and grandfather each placed a hand on his shoulder and a jolt shot through his body. Blue lightning arced from their fingertips into his flesh. He felt it flow into his pores and the electricity raced up his nervous system.

Clinching his eyes tightly shut, he waited until the sensations in his body ebbed.

Slowly, he opened his eyes to a new world. The blue light he saw when his kin touched him surrounded the tiny graveyard and a whitish-blue haze blazed from the three tombstones within the ancient walls. All the trees and plants glowed in the dark. Danny blinked and furiously rubbed his eyes trying to rid his vision of the haunting hues.

"See the island as we do son. You are now the guardian and nothing is allowed to pass the barrier of the cemetery walls except for you and whoever you choose when the time comes. We pass it down through the generations and you don't have to guard alone my son," his father said and walked into the middle of the graves.

"Then why don't you stay with me?" Danny said as tears streamed down his face.

"I'm dying. We both are and that's why we brought you here, to pass along your birthright. You are now the guardian and protector Danny. Remember, we'll both always love you," his father answered as he turned to the cemetery's entrance.

Danny watched his grandfather enter the cemetery and stand next to his son. A dark pool began seeping up from the soil around the pair. Holding hands, the two men sank into the murky water within the cemetery walls leaving Danny alone and confused.

***

Two Days Ago

He knew something was wrong when he saw the boat tied to the tree near the landing point. The locals knew the island was off limits and respected the sanctity of the place. The burial places around the area for the founders of White Creek were held in reverence and not to be trifled with. Local legends spoke of demons, sorcery, and witchcraft; but most laughed it off as superstition and hearsay.

Most people were wrong.

Danny knew better; he was charged with protecting a part of the town's heritage and someone had come to the island, violating the balance.

Someone threatened everything. Someone risked tearing down the barriers. Someone risked dooming them all. He pulled his small boat to the shore and stashed it behind the rock formation by the wooded island edge.

When he cut a proper trail five years ago to aid him on his treks back to the cemetery, he never imagined others would dare set foot on the island and use it. Tossed aside at the trail head he spied three beer bottles and a jacket. Walking toward the trail head, he bent over and picked up the jacket, a White Creek High letterman's jacket. Turning it around, his guts churned when he read the name emblazoned across the back in bright red letters, *KING*.

Damn boy, you should've known better, he thought and stormed off on the trail to the cemetery. Behind him, he swore he heard the bay roil and the waves crash harder against the island beaches. He also thought he heard... them.

His island eyes kicked in and everything took on its ethereal hues as he felt the energy pulsing through the land and the life on it. Every step closer to the clearing where the old stones laid made him anxious. A shift in the air already weighed on him. In all the years he'd been on the sacred ground, he'd never experienced the atmosphere as heavy and charged as it was now. Surveying the trees and plants along the trail, the normal blue and white colors were darkening and swirling around. Reds and blacks replaced the island's aura.

Whatever they've done, they've awakened it.

Danny broke into a run. In the distance he heard the laughing and the passionate cries coming from the clearing. A breeze began blowing across the island bringing the stench of weed, booze, and youthful lust. A humming reached his ears and he knew the land was charging itself, preparing to attack.

Six generations of King's had guarded the sacred island and on his watch it was going to all come tumbling down. His pace quickened and off in the distance, ahead of him on the trail, he swore for a moment he could see his father and grandfather and both hung their heads low, unable to look him in the eyes. Shame filled Danny's soul - shame and fear.

Danny scared the teens when he came from behind the row of pine trees. He smelled the salt water close around him on the cold island breeze and his heart skipped a beat when he found four teens fornicating on the old stone cemetery walls.

"Get down now!" he roared charging toward them.

The guys quickly backed up and pulled their pants up. The girls dropped down to the ground searching for their panties and pushing their skirts down off their hips.

"Damon! What the fuck are you doing?" Danny screamed.

"Dad... we... ah, yeah," Damon stammered. Defeat filled his voice because he knew the shit was going to hit the fan.

"And the rest of you! What would your parents think if they knew you were out here of all places and doing what you're doing? Come on, let's hurry, your folks are probably worried sick," Danny shouted and began to motion for the kids to follow him. The air shifted and he realized they didn't have much time.

Danny's pace increased the closer they came to the shore. The air began to reek and cooled until he saw his breath fan out in front of him each time he exhaled. Once they cleared the woods, his heart sank. The boat was torn apart and scattered along the shore. Planks littered the sands and the rope that once secured it to the tree was shredded. He shot a fast glance to the rocks and saw his boat still secure and hidden.

There's not enough room for all of us, he thought.

The girls screamed when they saw their boat's wreckage. One of them rushed over and grabbed a splintered piece from the rocks and shook her head in disbelief.

"Now what are we going to do!" she cried.

Danny looked out at the bay and froze. Damon started to step toward the water, but his father held him back.

"What, Dad? Let's get the hell out of here, you've scared Peggy and Hannah to death and you're freaking me out."

Then Damon saw it: three heads bobbing off the shoreline. They were black in the evening light and small red dots shone from them. A wave crashed on the rocks and the heads drew closer to the five standing on the island.

"Dad?" Damon asked, his voice full of fear.

"We have to go back," Danny whispered.

Damon's friend Kyle shook his girlfriend's hand off his arm and ran to the shore. Tossing his shirt to the ground, he stepped in the water.

"Kyle! Get back here!" his girlfriend Peggy screamed.

"Kyle, come back!" Damon shouted.

"It's too late son," Danny muttered and stood transfixed on the boy running out into the cold water.

Kyle rushed into the foamy surf and jumped into the froth. His arms broke back above the surface as he started to swim to town. Each stoke took him further from the island and the others could only watch and hope he reached the mainland.

***

He pushed his arms as fast as they could go and kicked his feet with all his might, but he didn't think he was getting closer to the docks. The beams from the lighthouse cut through the growing fog and when he turned his head to breathe, he saw them. Kyle counted three heads in the water and they all glared at him.

Oh, Jesus. They saw me.

Suddenly, his chest seized up like a giant fist squeezed

him tightly. Pushing through the pain, he drove his arms and legs to swim faster. Gasping, salt water splashed into his mouth and he choked on the taste.

I've won three swim titles, I can do this! He thought and focused on the shore.

The water began to thicken around him. He felt like he was swimming in a pool of Jell-O and each stroke became harder and harder. Fear pounded through him and the one place he could always find solace from the world was quickly becoming his enemy.

Opening his eyes to gauge his location in the bay, he found the fog had devoured the town and when he snuck a peek behind him, he realized the island had vanished too. He stopped and treaded water trying to get his bearings.

"Damon! Peggy! Hannah!" he called out as the waves lapped at his mouth. Salt water quickly filled his mouth and he spat it back out.

Nobody answered and even the lighthouse's horn had fallen silent.

"Shit, shit, shit," he muttered.

Deciding on a direction, he began to swim again. Something brushed past him in the water and he slowed. It felt like Peggy's fingertips running up his thigh when they made out, except it made him feel cold all over. Picking up speed again, the sensation happened a second time and lingered longer around his ankles. Panicking, he gave his arms and legs everything he had. His body sped through the black, further into the fog. Something grabbed his foot and he jerked to a halt in the water. Dipping beneath the surface, he pushed back up and fought for air. Three sets of red dots appeared before him.

A second tug took him under and he twisted quickly around, freeing himself. Before he could break the surface, water filled his lungs. He tried to cough, but he swallowed more instead. Kyle flinched as more hands took hold of his feet and yanked down—hard. Opening his eyes and looking upward toward the surface, he saw the shore getting further and further away.

They pulled him down for what seemed like miles. Tiny bubbles flew from his nose and he tried to hold what little breath he had left. His lungs seized and hitched one last time. Opening his mouth wide, it erupted in large bubbles and the last thing he saw was his final breath rocketing to the surface.

***

Danny knew once the fog rolled over Kyle he was gone. He looked over at his son and the two girls. Damon wrapped his arms around Hannah's shoulders and Peggy fell to her knees weeping loudly. Out on the water, the fog dissipated and Kyle was nowhere in sight.

"Come on, we have to get back to the cemetery," Danny said and rushed to the trail head.

"What are those things Dad?" Damon asked as the other three rushed to catch up to him.

Huffing, Danny stopped and turned to his son, "Don't ask what you don't want to know the answer to, son."

Damon reached out and shoved his father. Danny flinched in surprise and stared at his son.

"Why are you taking us back to the cemetery?"

"Because we have to make things right, now come on," Danny said and ran.

Within a few minutes they found themselves standing before the crumbling stone cemetery walls. A blue haze surrounded the three markers in the middle. Danny stepped closer to the entrance and the closer he got to the entryway, the muddier the ground became. He looked at the ground within the walls and saw it was becoming more and more saturated. Damon, Peggy, and Hannah stood by in silence and watched more water seep up from the ground around the graves.

Danny pulled a book from his pocket and frantically flipped through the pages. Finding the correct page, he skimmed the words looking for something, anything that would call off the dead men. Sighing, he closed the book and hung his head low.

"Dad? What is it?" Damon asked. He stepped closer to his father and started to feel uneasy. The look frozen on his father's face chilled him. He'd never witnessed a look like it on his father before.

"Over behind the third tree, there are some shovels. I want you to grab them and then we need to get to work," Danny answered. His voice sounded distant and despondent.

Damon rushed over behind the tree and found a large metal box. Flinging open the top, he found two shovels and a pick axe. Grabbing the lot, he hurried back to his father and the frightened girls and tossed them on the ground. They made a wet smacking sound when they hit the mud and began to sink. Water pooled around the tools and Damon backed away.

Wetness seeped into his shoes and an electric jolt shot through his system. Images flashed in his mind and he yanked his feet back away from the water. Shivers racked his body and his face fell slack.

"Damon, are you alright?" Hannah said and put her hand on his shoulder.

"NO!" He screamed and pushed her hand away. Suddenly everything on the island seemed… different.

Danny stood back and watched the scene. He knew what had transpired, what the water did to him. It showed him the truth about his family's legacy. It showed him the price to be paid. He wondered if he saw the island and the water like he did or if it only gave him a quick glimpse into his future or into his bloodline's past. He'd have plenty of time to teach him everything he'd need to know about the island and the history he was now tied to.

"Hannah, honey? I need you and Peggy to come here and help me dig in the cemetery," he said flatly and took up the pick axe.

Hannah slowly bent over to grab a shovel, never letting her eyes leave Damon. Peggy followed suit and took the last shovel from the deepening puddles on the ground.

"Put your hands in it," Damon ordered.

"Put them in what Damon?" Hannah asked. Her tone sounded weak and beaten.

"In the water! Put them in there now! I can't be the only one it talks to," he cried out.

The girls knelt down and placed their trembling hands in the brown muddy pools. They held their hands there for a few moments and pulled them out again. Damon hovered over them waiting for a sign they saw the horrible visions he faced, but neither looked shocked or repulsed. Both girls looked like nothing had happened.

"We need to dig in front of the three stones before the water rises in the cemetery," Damon said and walked through the gateway. The girls followed and Danny stayed back to watch.

***

The wind whipped harder through the trees and the deepening water chilled the three teens to their bones. Each gust cut through their jackets and every muscle burned from their labor. The hole before the markers grew wider and deeper with each shovel of dirt, but the dark water quickly seeped up from the soil to fill it in.

Hannah stopped, on the brink of exhaustion, and gazed into the black pool she stood in. Images swam through the ripples in the mirrored surface. Faces pushed up through the ink-like liquid and bared their teeth. Most opened their mouths in silent screams and faded back into the dark pools. Hannah stepped back and felt for the grave marker behind her. Her mouth hung open, but no words spilled forth.

Peggy noticed as Hannah slowly covered her mouth, her eyes widening as she gazed into the pool. Quickly, Peggy dropped her shovel and rushed to Hannah's side.

"Hannah? Hannah, can you hear me? What is it?" Peggy asked as she shook Hannah's shoulders.

"The water, in the water I saw them," she mumbled and pointed to the large pool in the shallow hole they dug before the markers.

Peggy knelt down and looked into the black muck filling the hole. The surface remained smooth as glass and she reached her finger out to touch it. Her finger slid into the pool and it caused a small ripple to form and move to the other side.

"Hannah, there's nothing here," she said.

Hannah screamed when a hand shot from the pool and latched onto Peggy's arm. Peggy tried to yank it back, but the arm tugged on her and pulled her in to her elbow. Screaming, she tried to roll away from the hole's edge and a second arm reached out and grabbed her leg.

Damon watched with a bemused smirk on his face. He'd seen the path, the righteous way he needed to take. He glanced at his father who stared at the scene with the same knowing look plastered on his face.

Hannah snapped out from her daze and grabbed Peggy's free hand and tried to pull her free. The water roiled and a column shot up and writhed in the air like a tentacle. Hannah gasped at the watery appendage and Peggy's hand slipped away from her. Swinging wildly, the tentacle smacked Hannah in the face and she stumbled backward, falling to the increasingly soggy ground.

The two hands dragged Peggy closer to the pool, her face stopping inches from the surface. Her reflection glared back at her with blazing red eyes and even though she didn't smile, one crossed the reflections lips revealing a row of sharp pointed teeth. From the corner of her eye, she spotted Damon step up beside her.

"Damon, I can't hold on much longer! Help me!" she pleaded.

"Here," Damon responded and swung the pick axe.

The pointed tip smashed into Peggy's skull. Hannah winced from the dull thud it made when it struck her friend, piercing her brain. Peggy's eyes crossed and a river of blood began flowing from the hole in the top of her head. The hands tugged on her and Damon let go of the pick axe's handle. Peggy's lifeless body slid into the inky pool and vanished beneath the surface.

"What have you done?" Hannah screamed at Damon through the sobs tearing through her body.

"Payment baby, payment," he responded smugly.

Hannah stood up and steadied herself on the markers. Damon reached his hand out to her and smiled his 'All-American' boy smile at her. She felt her guard go down and rushed over to hug him, the whole evening a blur in her head.

"Oh Damon," she muttered and let him wrap her in his arms.

"We have to pay baby, that's the nature of the beast. We all have to pay for the town," he whispered in her ear and gave her a quick peck on the cheek.

Next to them, the water swirled and the faces raced to the surface. Dozens of them broke through and then dove back into the ichor. Damon saw the parade of the forefathers… and pushed.

Hannah felt like she was falling backward in slow

motion. She'd felt safe in Damon's arms even after what he did to Peggy; she craved the comfort at the moment. She felt weak and used watching his lips form a maniacal grin... a knowing grin. Closing her eyes, she splashed into the pool and felt the multitude of hands grab her and pull. Her back struck the bottom, but the hands tugged harder and she felt her body sink into the ground. Opening her eyes to take one last look, she saw Peggy smiling beside her... then Peggy opened her mouth revealing her razor teeth.

Hannah tried to scream, but the black sludge filled her mouth, silencing her forever.

***

Danny stood by and watched as his son raised his arms in victory. He'd never been more proud of the boy.

I wonder if it's my time to go and leave him in charge, join my father and grandfather.

He noticed the water didn't dissipate after the sacrifices were offered to the founders. The fog began to pour from the cemetery and fill the space within its walls.

"Damon! Get out of there now!"

Damon saw the tendrils of white mist creep around his ankles. The cold he felt from touching the wispy fingers broke his paralysis and he ran for the gateway. He saw his father and ran over to him on the edge of the clearing.

"Dad, what is that?"

"It should have gone away! We gave it three lives for three of the tethered souls," he said in disbelief.

Then it hit him like a ton of bricks, Damon had violated

the sanctity of the cemetery and the markers within. He had to pay also.

Danny gazed upon his son and he felt the island call to him to pay the owed amount. Damon stood before him, his only son and heir to his legacy. In his mind the island's aura shifted to an angry red and the fog bank forming around the markers began churning.

"Damon," Danny whispered, "I have a boat hidden on the shore. When I say go, we run as fast as we can to get it and get off this fucking island."

Damon nodded.

"Go."

Father and son tore away from the clearing and ran down the path as fast as they could go, neither one looking back to see if the fog gave chase. Branches swatted them and left welts in their skin. Water seeped from the ground and they both began to slip in the mud. Staying focused, they looked forward and saw the rock formation where the boat lay hidden.

"Damon, quick let's get her in the water!"

They both picked up the boat and ran to the shore. The waves increased as they dove into the water. Danny pushed Damon over the side into the boat. Staying in the water, he swam toward the town pushing the boat out of the shallow area surrounding the island.

Damon looked out and saw the three heads in the water. "Dad, quick, take my hand!"

Danny reached up and took his son's hand and pulled

himself over the side.

"Thanks boy," he said huffing from swimming against the crashing waves.

Grabbing the oars, they paddled and never looked back.

***

Now

Danny heard Damon snore and mumble something under his breath. The town had been on edge since the other night and Danny knew it was his fault. Sensing the spirits anger, he also felt them give him the opportunity to make amends and pay.

In his mind, he heard his father and grandfather plead with him, but their spectral voices fell on deaf ears. Some people had already left town and only a few families here and there remained. The fog rolled closer to the docks and he could hear the cries of the damned souls trapped in it. Occasionally, a face would show through; sometimes it was Kyle and in others, it would be Hannah or Peggy he was staring at.

Still, he sat and drank.

Damon sat down beside him and gazed out at the fog creeping across the cursed water.

"This is my fault Dad," he said and buried his face in his hands.

"No, it's mine and mine alone."

"But I killed them and gave them to it," he managed to

say between sobs.

"We all pay a price in this town Damon. The cursed ones paid theirs like we all have to pay ours. We all have to face responsibility for our actions, son."

Damon stood up and looked over the rock face cliff down to the docks and the water. The bay usually experienced little waves from the current, but they tore through the docks and crashed into the fishing boats anchored down tossing them like toys in a bath tub. He stepped out further and felt the cliff give a little beneath him.

The rocks behind him crunched and Damon turned around to see his father standing there staring at him.

"We all have a price to pay," he muttered and reached his hands out.

The Iceberg

Patrick Van Slyke

A large, exhausted man gingerly pushed open the door to the Oyster Cage, a warped, salt crusted pub about as close to the wharf as you could get. It wasn't for tourists. It was for sailors; period.

Craig found the patrons staring at him in shock. The large man looked like he had been torn to pieces.

"Craig! For God's sakes man, what's happened? Where're your brothers?" Stirge came around from behind the bar and guided his friend to a stool near the door. Another friend near Craig pushed him a fresh beer without a thought.

In two gulps the beer was gone. Craig, a giant of a man, white as a ghost, covered in burns and frost bites, looked around without seeing.

"It's coming. It followed me here. It took my brothers. First Coil, then Cory. Stella is gone. So is Jemma. It's gonna take us too. See, it ain't supposed to be here. It got caught here somehow. It ain't even from anywhere. But it likes us. It likes it here. It says it's an angel. Coil said that its name is Camarothud. But it...

He looked down at the bar and started to sob quietly. "We're already dead."

***

Even in the dark, Cory felt pride at the lines of his twenty-eight footer center console, 'Jemma,' named after his first real love. It was fitting his first girl should proudly identify his only constant adult love. She was faithful, strong, loving, and beautiful.

"I still don't know why we got to go out now," Craig yawned. Craig was Cory's younger brother but he was big, way bigger than this brother at six-four and two-hundred twenty. But Craig was a teddy-bear and wouldn't hurt anybody unless they deserved it and even then they really, really had to deserve it.

Cory was the driver. He had started 'Three Brothers Seas' and it was he who had made it a success. They had started as simple fishermen but with Cory's drive, Coil's brains and Craig's muscles they had been unstoppable. By the time the triplets had turned thirty, they had five boats; three fishers and two cruisers. Soon, Coil promised, they would be able to buy another twenty-eight footer, cash. Cory shook his head. Cash. The Lord had been good to them.

"Coil was supposed to dock around midnight and I got a bad feeling. On his last transmission he said he saw something."

"Aw, he was probably just busy counting numbers in his head," the giant man said as he prepped the ship. "What'd he say he saw?"

"That's what's bugging me," Cory said firing up the

twin-outboards, his voice rising automatically to compensate. "He said he saw an iceberg."

Craig threw back his shaggy head and laughed loud enough to be heard at sea.

He loosed the last line and jumped into the craft. "Wait, you're serious?"

"Yah," his brother confirm grimly. "He said he was going to check it out."

"You think he might have been hallucinating?"

"I dunno, but I ain't going to wait for the coast guard. We know these waters better than them anyway. I got his position and he's not moving. He's about thirty miles out."

"That's a ways out, that's for sure, if something's wrong. What the hell would make him think he saw an iceberg?"

"God only knows. Coil ain't stupid. And he didn't say he saw an iceberg, he said he saw something 'like' an iceberg and he was going to check it out. That was the last transmission."

"But we got his locator beacon," Craig said, pointing at the blinking green light.

"Yah, we got his locator beacon. That's where we are headed right now."

"Well, now I understand why it couldn't wait," Craig agreed grimly as the outboards roared to life, pushing Jemma though the briny chop. "What did he take out?"

"One of the trawlers. Um… 'Stella.'"

The night was dark and once past the harbor markers it was like a different world. Their running lights were the best money could buy but they were still left with just a small puddle of illumination. The moon was a better guide, but it was in the process of being devoured by incoming clouds.

"How many did Coil have on 'Stella'?"

"Uh," Cory typed into his table, the light making his face look eerily like a corpse. "He had four men with him. Two new kids, but he also had James and Rick."

"James and Rick are good men," Craig said more to himself than anyone.

"Yah, they know the water and they know 'Stella.' The new kids, I don't know, some in-lander name of Davis, and a college boy, Frank, they should be fine. Seemed liked they had no trouble with shutting up and listening."

Craig left the console and made his way to the bow. It was cold and the wind was picking up, but nothing unusual.

"What's out there Craig?"

"Nuthin. Smooth sailing but we got a squall coming in. Nothing big. We'll only hit the edge. Weird smell, Cory. Nothing I've ever smelled before."

"You need me to slow down?"

"Naw, nothing like that."

"Seaweed?"

"Naw." Cory was the best navigator there was on the southern California coast. Often, other captains would request his help by name in searches. Cory never let go the wheel, no matter how slow or how clear the water. He navigated by feel. He would have known about any seaweed or obstacle before his brother. He asked simply to gather info. Navigation was about information.

Cory told everyone, "Pay attention to details. If you pay attention to details you can never get lost, never get break down, you always come home." He was looking to Craig for details.

"It isn't seaweed. I've never smelt it before. It's gross. How close are we?"

"Close, around two or three miles," he said, pulling back the throttle a bit. The black was now complete. They were an isolated pearl beating back the ever encroaching dark.

"Jemma two-four, four," Craig heard his brother call. "Jemma two-four, four to Stella four-four, one. Coil, are you there?"

Cory called and called but didn't have much hope of an answer. They were too close. Coil's radio was down, he could not answer or he would not answer. Those were the possible explanations. Cory didn't like any of them.

"I smell it now," Cory yelled to his brother, bringing the engines almost to idle. "What the hell is that?"

"It doesn't smell natural, Cory. It doesn't smell organic."

Cory brought the boat to a stop and killed the engines. The only sound was the whisper soft slap of gentle waves against the hull.

"Something isn't right," Cory said, grabbing the

mounted hand controlled spotlight and began to scan the area around the boat. "What's in front of us Craig?"

"Nothing. I've never heard a quieter night."

"Or seen one darker. It's like the light can't cut into it. But there is something in front of us. I can feel it. Grab a light and see what you can find." Cory started the boat and began to inch forward.

"Nothing, Cory. You're off this time. Just water and…" there was a pause. Craig brought the boat to a stop again. "I… I see something. It looks like an oil slick. The smell… I think the smell is coming from this shit."

Cory cut the engine and walked to the front of the boat. "I see it. What the hell color is that stuff?"

Craig grabbed a hook pole and slapped it out just far enough to touch the slick. He grunted. "It looks almost clear, but… it looks like there… Jesus! Did you see that?"

The slick had reacted violently when the pole had touched it, jerking back out of range as if it could feel the hook. A wail, almost too quiet to hear, echoed through the dark night.

Cory's eyes were sharper. "It's milky and seems to have veins like a plant or something. But it ain't no plant I ever saw."

"One thing is for sure. It didn't like being touched. You hear that noise it made?"

"Yah, sounded like a gull being pulled under but worse. Something ain't right. This ain't no ordinary night."

Cory turned and made his way back through the ink to

the isolated glow of the console.

"It says we're almost right on top of him."

"Coil!" Craig yelled in his huge voice. "Ahoy, Stella!" No answer. He turned back to his brother. We either lower a dingy or we power in. What's your call?"

"How thick would you guess that slick is?"

"No more than an inch, if that. And it pulled back when I touched it."

Cory powered the engines to life and began to inch forward.

"We're okay," Craig yelled. "It's pulling back, making way for us. It don't want to be touched."

Cory looked behind them with the spotlight and saw that his brother was right. They were cutting a channel through the milky substance and he was unconsciously relieved to see that it wasn't closing behind them.

"Cory! Cut the engines and get up here. You better see this."

"You see Stella?"

"Yah, and I see her iceberg, too."

Engines cooling, Cory rushed to the bow. "What the hell...?" he began and then stuttered to a stop. Stella was tilted at about a thirty degree angle, bow up. She was pushed up against the 'iceberg' and seemed to be held their by the milky fluid that floated on the surface of the ocean.

"She's taking on water in the stern," Craig said numbly.

"Yah, either that or she's run up on something. Either way she's in trouble. No lights on. And that ain't no iceberg." The formation stuck out of the water like a small mountain peak, the sides broken and cut by holes, crevices, outcroppings; it was completely asymmetric. "It looks like black rock or metal ore or some shit."

"Stella ain't got no lights on and that ain't good. That stuff… that slimy shit seems to be making a… I don't know, like a cocoon around her. It smells like some kind of chemical. Maybe it drained the batteries."

"It's possible," Cory said, squinting his eyes. "Okay, this is something I've never seen and I've seen everything. I don't think dad ever saw anything like this either. I think he would have told us."

"Nah, he never said anything like this…"

"Okay, okay, shut up a moment," Cory said bringing his fists to the sides of his head. Craig knew he wasn't talking to him but to his own brain. He was trying to analyze what was happening. Coil was the deductive one. Cory was used to making quick decisions based on feeling.

"Run back there, Craig, and see if that shit is trying to close in on us."

As Craig ran off Cory began to speak softly to himself. "Okay, it isn't ice. Got to be rock, but maybe porous or hollow so it will float. That shit in the water must be coming from it cause it's pulling Stella closer and closer." He brought the main spotlight to bear and pulled up his binoculars. "It looks like it is covered with some kind of ash or dust, and there's… is that…?"

"It's still open behind us," Craig said as he came jogging forward.

Cory handed him the binoculars. "Look right there by her stern. Where I got the light pointed. What do you see?"

Craig squinted through the binoculars and was silent for a moment. "Either I'm going crazy or there are footprints in that dust leading to that crevice in the rock."

"Yah, that's what I see too. Okay, we pull back and take a dingy in. I don't want that shit trying to grab up Jemma, too. What do you think? One of us or both?"

"Both, Cory," he said as if his brother was slow. "We're brothers. We stick together."

"Yah, both. You're right. I'm gonna pull her back."

The engines roared to life again and without incident Cory had them at about one hundred meters beyond the scum. They could just barely make out the rock. Cory set the engines to hold GPS position and then went to help Craig drop the dingy.

Jemma's dingy had a small outboard so they didn't have to paddle but in a way, he wished they did. The motor was nothing like Jemma's but it was still loud and it was like a siren notifying anybody listening that they were coming. This time the slime did not make way for them but split as they cut through. Now they could tell the cry of unearthly pain was coming from the slick. There was no doubt that it was reacting to their approach.

Craig put his hands over his ears. "It's horrible!" he cried. "Make it stop! It's driving me crazy!"

It was making Cory lose his grip on reality as well. The sound, though low, was a cry like nothing ever heard on earth before. It made Cory want to laugh and cry and kill himself all at the same time.

"But brother's stick together!" he screamed and, opening his eyes he found that Craig, eyes wide, was about to jump overboard. "No Craig! Brothers stick together!"

"Brothers stick together," he parroted dumbly. "Yah, brothers stick together!"

Just as the words were out of his mouth the dingy pulled into an open area of water between the slime and the black rock-like formation that held Stella helpless. The cry faded away but it had left a scar in Cory that would never go. This could not be something natural to their world.

"Find something to fasten us on to," he hissed to his brother as he grabbed two high-powered flashlights.

The rock, or metal or whatever it was burnt their hands. It was hot and cold at the same time.

"It's freezing," Cory hissed pulling his hand back, "but it also feels like it has an electrical charge or something that burns. We need gloves and our rubbers."

With thick gloves on his hands and rubber boot covers, Cory was able to pull himself up onto the jagged ledge where they had seen the footprints.

"Those are footprints for sure," Craig said, coming up beside his brother, shining his light down. "Looks like all five of 'em went down there."

"Eh?"

"Yah, check it out, you can see five different prints easy. They abandoned their ship."

"It can't be. Coil would have called before abandoning ship. Coil would never abandon. Come on, let's have a look at Stella."

With each step they stirred up more of the dust covering every surface of the rock formation. It had the same acidic chemical smell that the sea scum had only much more intense. There was also a faint hint of rotting flesh. It smelled like a lab experiment gone seriously wrong.

"We're not going to be able to get in there," Craig said through the sleeve of his shirt held over his mouth to keep the dust out.

It looked like he was right. The milky, slightly luminescent film had pulled the ship tight to the rock and seemed to be in the process of slowly crushing it against the dense formation, but it was the same scum that was going to keep them out of the wheel house. It was engulfing the ship, covering every possible entrance.

Cory pulled his long, wicked knife from his boot and gingerly walking as close to the boat as he could get, tried to cut his way onto the ship. The effect was startling. The wail they had encountered before burst loudly around them making them both cry out and cover their ears. Where Cory had cut the growth a milky fluid splashed on his rubbers and began to smoke as it burnt into the tough material.

"Get away from there!" Craig screamed, eyes wide as his sanity threatened to snap.

Cory didn't need any more urging. Stumbling backward

into his brother's arms, he yanked off his rubber boot covers. At one point he touched the viscous liquid and screamed in pain. It burnt at his skin like acid but seemed to have spent most of its energy on his boots and soon he was just left with a bad burn on his left hand.

With the cessation of the attack on the oily mucus the cry began to die down and it finally faded away, leaving the unnatural silence of the black night. The two brothers found themselves hugging each other close, on their knees, tears pouring down their cheeks.

"We got to get out of here!" Craig cried.

As much as Cory wanted to agree, he just couldn't. Stella was gone but his brother might still be alive. "We have to find Coil and the crew," he said, steeling himself and standing. Yanking his brother up, he continued. "Stella is a lost cause but there is no reason to think that Coil or his crew is not still alive."

"Come on, Cory! They would have come running if they had heard that!" He began to pull his brother toward the dingy. "They're dead. Can't you feel it? This place... ate them. We got to go!"

"No!" Cory shouted, shaking his brother off. "They might be trapped or hurt. Brothers stick together, remember. Go if you want, but I am following these tracks to see where my brother is."

Craig looked like a caged animal, eyes wide and for one second Cory thought he even might take a swing at him, but finally the insanity left his eyes and he let out a breath. "Right, brothers stick together. Let's go."

The brothers turned their lights toward the cleft opening into the rock. It was jagged, with sharp edges but fairly large and even Craig could enter with ease. The bottom of the crack seemed unusually smooth, making walking easy.

Just inside the cave it seemed that they had left the confines of the world they had known and been transported somewhere... else. Somewhere unnatural. The cave opened up a bit and they saw that it sloped down slightly and seemed to twist to the right. Shining his light down, Cory saw that they footprints were leading them farther in.

"Man I don't like this," he muttered to himself.

"It's like a bad dream," his brother agreed.

Slowly, almost on top of each other, the brothers began to make their way farther into the enigmatic formation. They found themselves trying to walk in the steps of the others to keep the dust from being disturbed.

Craig covered his nose and mouth again. "Man the smell is getting worse." It was, Cory agreed silently. It was taking on more of a rotten meat smell now. He fought to keep his hand from shaking.

To cover his tremors, he flashed his light for a closer look at the walls. They seemed less natural now and more as if they had been carved. They were not smooth, but they were losing their jagged edges, making walls of black bubbles of all sizes and shapes, frozen in the hard rock. "This is a strange formation," Cory said, jumping at the loudness of his own voice in the absolute quiet.

"That's stranger," his brother said; point his light toward the roof of the cave. Without notice it had become smooth too, like the floor and at the edge, where the wall met the ceiling was a row of what looked to be carved symbols.

"Oh, God," Cory moaned. The sight of the ornate hieroglyphs burnt into his eyes, making his head pound and he felt like he was going to throw up. "What is that?" he gaged, taking his eyes away from the writing.

"I don't know but we don't belong here. This," he gestured around them, "doesn't belong here. This ain't natural, Cory. I don't think it's from this earth."

"I am beginning to agree with you, Craig. Tell you what, it looks like there might be a light just beyond that bend down there. Let's go and have a look around the corner. If it's Coil, great, we grab him and go. If not, we bail and wait for the coast guard. Sound okay?"

"Okay," he said, sounding anything but okay.

Without another word they began to walk silently down the unnatural hallway. It seemed to stretch farther and farther, like in a bad dream but after what seemed like an eternity they reached the gentle turn and with a few more shuffling steps, they looked into a dimly lit cavern. If it was possible, the cave was more disturbing than the hallway. The unnerving writing continued on around the perfectly circular room, only here they seemed to glow with a watery green light. The walls were still bubbly looking but now the bubbles seemed to have more shape, almost looking like animals, humans and unimaginable creatures encased in the black rock. The only other thing in the room was a large circular hole in the center going straight down.

"Okay," Craig said, "let's get out of here and wait for the coast guard."

"Wait a minute!" Cory hissed, making his way to the hole in the floor. "What if they fell in there?"

"How the hell is someone going to fall in there? They'd have to be blind."

"Jesus, Craig!" Cory hissed. "He's your fucking brother!

Cory took another look at the hole. It was about ten feet in diameter, easily large enough for the largest man to fit through, and the smooth surface around it sloped down into it. Small rivulets had been cut into the rock all the way around, making it look like some kind of maw. He inched forward trying to look down.

His feet slipped and he almost went in. Before he could even react a ham sized fist grabbed him by the collar, stopping his momentum with no effort at all.

"Jesus," he panted, looking back at his brother. "Thank you!"

"It's time to go," Craig hissed back.

"Almost."

"Cory…"

"No, Craig, I can almost see down there. Just hold on to me. I thought I saw something. Coil might be down there. Look, I'll be safe enough. Just don't let go."

"No Cory, we got to…"

"Cory?" a voice came whispering out of the hole in the sickly cavern.

"I told you!" Cory said to his brother, a mad look in his

eyes.

"Cory is that you?" The voice was Coil's, that was for sure, but Craig thought there was a bubbly, liquid sound to it. It terrified him.

"Coil!" Cory laughed. "I knew we would find you. Are you okay?"

"Okay?" the voice bubbled.

"Yah. Are your mates down there with you?"

"Oh, we're all down here. Would you like to come down?"

"Would I like to…? What the hell are you talking about? Stella is destroyed. We got to get you out of there. How the hell did you get down there anyway?"

"We got to go!" Craig whispered.

"What the fuck is the matter with you?" Cory yelled, twisting in Craig's grasp. "That's our brother down there. We got to get him out."

"We don't want to come out, Cory," the wet voice dribbled up the hole. "We like it down here. There are lots of us down here."

"What are you talking about Coil?" Cory asked, inching forward. "We got to get off this thing and get home."

"This isn't a thing, Cory," the voice bubbled gleefully. "It's an angel. An angel from another place. Somewhere not here. It got stuck here but it likes this world and it likes us. And soon we will be up there, in the hall of trophies."

"He's sick, probably in shock," Cory said to himself

inching a bit forward so he could shine his light farther down. "I can't see you Coil. Can you see the light?"

"Yes, but I don't like it. We are part of the dark now. Everything is clean in the dark. We like it. You'll like it to. Come on down. The angel can show you how to feel. I never knew what it was to really feel and as soon as I am stripped clean, I'll be a trophy."

Cory turned toward Craig. "We got to get him…"

But he was unable to finish. The room gave a violent jerk and, caught unaware, both brothers failed to act. With a cry Cory slid into the hole.

"No!" Craig cried but he could get no closer.

He heard his brother wail as he fell and fell. Then there was a sickening wet thud.

"Fuck me," his brother said from below. "I'm okay Craig. I landed on something soft. You'll have to go and get the rope and…"

"Cory!" the voice bubbled and gibbered. "You've joined us. This is the Angel Camarothud. He is from beyond our universe. We are a part of him now."

"No… no," Cory said dully and then screamed with such terror and pain that Craig was frozen, unable to move. "Oh, look," Cory said in the same bubbly voice. "The skin comes right off. He's right, Craig. I have never felt before. Come down here with us."

Craig turned and ran. They were in a monster and there was nothing he could do for his brothers now. The angel bucked and shook, trying to get Craig into the hole but he was too far out of the room.

He did fall and where his skin touched the living rock his skin burned and froze. But Craig was unaware of the damage he was taking. He was running on survival instincts now. He had to get out.

Once again, the hallway seemed to elongate only now it seemed to shrink in diameter too. But no matter how it shook it could not stop Craig. He ran on adrenaline and shock. Once he exited the crevasse he stopped to catch his breath and looked around.

"No!" he cried when he saw that the dingy had been absorbed by the ocean slime. Stella was in worse condition. He saw the running lights of Jemma but...

There was still a small pool of sea that was clear between the formation and the slime. Looking out he saw that, for some reason, the floating crap had not filled in the path Jemma had taken. If he dove in and swam maybe he could make it to the clear path before he had to come up for air. It only took a second to decide and like a shot he dove into the ocean.

His dive had been perfect and, being a strong swimmer, he knew he could easily make it to Jemma's path. But as he swam, under the scum, he saw what was at the bottom of what Coil had called Camarothud. It was like an iceberg in that only about ten percent of it was above water, but below the waterline it changed. Rock became ghastly gelatinous flesh, alive with tentacles and gills and great mouths and beaks. It reached for Craig. It wanted it him to become part of it. He swam.

Craig swam as hard as he could. He was aware of the

tentacles reaching for him but he did not look back. Every second was an eternity and he kept expecting to feel the acidic clasp of the beast but it never came. When he could hold it no longer he surfaced and found that he was almost to Jemma. It looked like the monster had given up on him.

On board Jemma, without thought Craig turned the ship and headed toward land. He was unaware of his surroundings. He could not get the vision of what he had seen underwater out of his head.

He headed for home. The navy would kill that thing, he told himself, not really believing it. He was about half way to the dock when he realized that the monster was following him. He could not get away. "Maybe he should go live in Wyoming," he thought. But he knew it wouldn't work. He would never be able to get away. Camarothud liked it here.

Moon in Submergence

Timothy C. Hobbs

Dr. Randolph Zaetz held the phone receiver next to his ear while he tapped the remains of tobacco from his well-used pipe into a desk ashtray. The ashtray was a sculpted porcelain monkey dressed in a white medical coat; the monkey wore a stethoscope and gazed with curiosity at a human skull gripped in its paw. Zaetz's colleague, Paul Addison, was on the phone line.

"I know you have an ungodly schedule, Randolph," Addison said, "but I think you would find this patient an interesting referral."

"Under normal circumstances, I'd be happy to see him, Paul," Zaetz replied as he packed a new plug of cherry tobacco into his pipe. "However, I have that seminar next week, and then it's Thanksgiving right after. Don't think I could squeeze him in until the first week of December."

There was a pause and an audible sigh. "Randolph, he won't make it that long. I've done all I can do with my therapy. He needs an expert in sleep disturbances. You're the best and most convenient referral I can think of."

"But he's not physically ill, right?"

"Not critically, but his condition is deteriorating due to sleep deprivation."

Zaetz tapped the glass desk top with a pen and then remarked, "I still don't understand the urgency."

"Please, Randolph. I know you can help him. You're the expert when it comes to sleep disorders."

Zaetz had published five papers on sleep disturbances, and Paul knew it was Zaetz's Achilles' heel.

Zaetz scanned the desk top computer for a look at his patient schedule. "Hmm, I can work him in this Monday at one p.m., Paul, but he must be punctual. I have to meet our guest speaker for the seminar. Her flight arrives at three thirty. I also have to confirm the hotel accommodations for the other colleagues arriving on Monday."

"I'll see that he keeps the appointment. Thanks, Randolph, I owe you one."

"Oh, Paul, send his chart over. You know how Fridays are. I'm apt to forget by the end of the day that your patient will be coming in. I don't want to face the man cold on Monday. I'd prefer a good look at his medical history."

***

The chart arrived just after noon. Zaetz normally made no appointments between four and five p.m. That was his wind down time and reserved for recovery from the trials and troubles brought in by patients. But today Zaetz would go against his established routine and study the record Paul Addison had sent him: the case of Robert Adams, a thirty four year old male on a road to physical burnout from lack of sleep.

A late minute drop-in, however, forced Zaetz to look at the chart on his way home instead of in the solitude of his office. His plans wouldn't allow him to stay any later than five that day, so he had to read Robert Adams' case file amid the noisy, irritating commuter train jumble.

Zaetz got a seat by the window to keep prying eyes away. It wouldn't do having a passenger privy to another's medical history. After a few pages, it was evident that Robert Adams was suffering from nocturnal emissions; a.k.a. 'wet dreams.' Zaetz couldn't suppress a grin. It was not the fact Adams suffered from wet dreams that caused the problem with his sleep, it was the frequency. The man had them nightly, sometimes as many as three. This had been going on for almost two months now.

The next bit of information brought a wider grin to Zaetz face: Robert's wife Sandra tended to be helpful and supportive of her husband's problem—that is until the incidences didn't stop and increased in number. Sandra finally had enough of semen staining the bed or dousing her back. In a no win competition with a supernatural dream lover rather than a human rival, Sandra's jealousy and frustration overcame what good nature she had once possessed. "Who the hell are you screwing?" was Sandra's question just before she packed her bags and headed out the door. Sandra had added as she stormed away, "I'll come back when you stop fucking that dream bitch! Not one day before!" Sandra's quotes were written on the margins of the hospital chart in red ink, which a bred a habit of Paul Addison's that particularly irked Zaetz's meticulous nature. The distraction of reading them, the tiresome prattle of the crowded car, and the constant clickity clackity of the moving train put a pounding headache between Zaetz's eyes. He closed the folder on this almost comical set of circumstances, shook his head in exasperation, leaned back and breathed in a lung full of the stale human smell around him. He would worry about Robert Adams on Monday. It didn't seem that important a case after all.

***

The following Monday, Robert Adams lay on the dark leather couch in Zaetz's office. His physical appearance was shocking. Zaetz's older brother Thomas and his return home from a long tour in Viet Nam came to mind as Zaetz gazed at Robert Adams. Before he had left for the war, Thomas Zaetz was the picture of health: a stone hard Marine ready for battle. On returning, Thomas had resembled a concentration camp survivor: haggard, thin, eyes circled with dark memories and terror. Robert Adams had that same look.

"Each dream is the same," Adams sighed. "All the elements constantly repeat themselves. Didn't Doctor Addison tell you this?"

"I always like to hear the problems first hand," Zaetz remarked as he made a note on his legal pad—EXTREME SLEEP DEPRIVATION. "So much can be lost from a second party's interpretation."

Adams sighed again, as if retelling the facts was an even heavier weight. "It starts with water. Always the water. I'm in my childhood room. Everything there is as I remember it: the baseball and football pennants on the wall, the desk in the corner, the shelf holding model cars and the Aurora Famous Monster figures.

"It's a boy's room, but I am my present age lying there in the bed. I feel the cold water surrounding me. I am under it; the room is flooded. The odd thing is nothing floats. Everything in the room stays in place like it's been nailed down. And there I am naked in bed. And I'm breathing the water like it's air.

"On my right there is an open window. A full moon glows in shimmering waves through it. It's a moon in submergence.

"I'm not alone in the room. A figure stands silhouetted by the window. It's a woman. She wears a thin white gown. I can see that she wears nothing under it.

"Her body is beautiful, lithe in form with sculptured breasts. Her erect nipples press at the night gown's lining. She turns to me. Her face is shadowed but I catch the flash of a smile. She moves her hands slowly down her body; they pass over her breasts until she reaches the patch of dark shade between her legs. A moan escapes her. She whispers something that I can't hear. She pulls the gown over her head, moves to the bed, and lies down beside me. Her body is bathed in moonlight. Her dark hair falls in a mass of curls around her shoulders.

"I am aware of a painful erection. I try to reach out but find my body is paralyzed. The woman then crawls on top of me. The soft radiant light reflects her face under the water. She is beauty incarnate. The Venus. The Madonna. Perfection molded into flesh. A thin line of bubbles outlines her mouth like a string of tiny pearls.

"She whispers again and this time I hear her. She says 'Mother' and grips my erection and guides it into her. And that's when I ejaculate with such force that it wakes me up.

I'm covered in semen. I'm left exhausted and drained.

"This happens more than once in the same night. I don't have to tell you what a strain it is on my health... and my marriage. Unfortunately, on several occasions, I've ejaculated on my sleeping wife."

Zaetz wiped a thin line of sweat from his forehead and then noticed an uncomfortable fullness between his legs. Damned if Adams' story hadn't given him a hard-on.

"But I suppose you read about my wife leaving me in the chart," Adams continued. "She thinks I'm having an affair, even if it is only in my dream."

Zaetz grimaced and crossed his legs. "In a way, Mr. Adams, she may be right."

"That's silly. It's only a dream."

"But one that ends in an all too real... emission, especially for your wife."

"Yes, but..."

Zaetz put his pad down and stood up. "I've strayed from the real issue of your sleep disturbance here, Mr. Adams. I apologize for that. We'll discuss the domestic repercussions after we find out how to make your nights better, agreed?"

"That's why I'm here." Adams sat up and leaned back; he rubbed his eyes as if to erase the fatigue.

"Do you mind?" Zaetz asked as he held up his pipe. "It helps my concentration, but I wouldn't want the smoke to bother you."

"Not at all," Adams said and patted his shirt pocket.

"Got a pack of Marlboro Lights right here."

"Feel free to smoke in this office, Mr. Adams," Zaetz commented and placed a separate ashtray on the coffee table in front of the couch. "I'm not the type to reserve the habit for myself."

Adams pulled out a Bic lighter and lit up a cigarette as Zaetz continued his conversation through a warm cloud of pipe smoke. "You said this dream woman whispered the word 'Mother.' In what context did she use it?"

"I'm not sure I understand what you're getting at."

"Why do you think she said 'Mother'?"

"Hey, I know the first thing you shrinks think of is that mother Oedipus thing, but if you think the word 'mother' in the dream refers to my own, forget it."

"Why so?"

Adams shook his head and ground out his cigarette. He leaned back wearily, a curl of yellow-white smoke flowed in tendrils from his nostrils. "The woman may say 'mother,' but her actions are not anywhere close to being motherly. At least not like any I've known, including my own." Adams smiled and said, "You guys."

Picking up his legal pad, Zaetz wrote down *'patient does not believe he is having symbolic intercourse with his mother. Check on references to forces of maternal origins'*.

"Very well," Zaetz said and placed the legal pad back on his desk. "Tell me how you feel about being under water in the dream."

"In the dream it doesn't bother me. And that's strange

because I am deathly afraid of being under water."

"Any particular reason for that fear? Something that happened to you or someone close to you?"

"Yeah, to me. I almost drowned when I was a kid."

Zaetz sat back down. Tapping tobacco from his pipe into the monkey ashtray, he asked, "Would you like to tell me about that incident?"

"Wish I could." Adams leaned forward and placed his head in his hands and rested his elbows on his knees. "My near drowning incident is all a blank spot up. The only thing I can recall about that day is when I woke up in a hospital bed. All the details before that just seem to have been erased."

"Maybe I can speak to your parents about it. Sometimes our loved ones are reluctant to open the box concealing a hurt. But they may talk to me."

"No," Adams said. "My parents died within a year of each other."

"Sorry." Zaetz made another note on the legal pad and then continued. "Do you live in the city, Mr. Adams?"

"No, we have a condo close to the ocean."

"That doesn't seem to be compatible with a fear of drowning."

"Believe me, I don't particularly like being near the water, but my wife loves it, especially strolling down the beach."

"How long have you been there?"

"A little over six months. I was transferred back to San

Diego. I'm from here originally."

"I see." Zaetz glared at his watch. The session time was almost over and he needed to prepare for the next patient. "Our time is about up today. Will you be able to make a follow up appointment?"

"Since we didn't solve anything, I guess I have no choice."

"Oh, I think we covered some important ground, Mr. Adams. I think your near drowning experience may have more to do with your problem than you know. How do you feel about hypnosis?"

"Hypnosis? Does that really work?"

"I think I can use hypnosis to pull out those memories of your near drowning. It's actually a very common practice in my field."

Adams didn't care if he had to swing a sack of owl shit over his head during an eclipse. If it would help him get a full night's sleep, let Zaetz send him back to embryonic memories if need be.

"Okay, why not," Adams said.

Zaetz frowned. "I detect skepticism in your voice, Mr. Adams. You must come with an open mind for a successful therapeutic session. You must put away preconceived notions of side show hucksters and charlatans."

"No skepticism here, doc." Adams stood up from the couch. "When should I come back?"

"Let me see." Zaetz sat at his desk and pulled up his schedule on the computer screen. "Normally my secretary would set this up, but I think you need to be scheduled as soon as possible. I have my seminar this Tuesday, Wednesday, Thursday, and Friday morning. How about two p.m. this Friday afternoon?"

"Works for me." Before leaving, Adams added, "I don't seem to have any kind of normal schedule these days anyway."

Zaetz made a final note after Adams left: *patient is extremely petulant due to lack of sleep; check with Katherine on legends of maternal origins.* Zaetz sat the legal pad down and let out a little laugh. His erection was still throbbing.

***

Dr. Katherine Phillips was an old acquaintance. Zaetz had shared classes with her at Berkley as well as doctorate studies at U.C.L.A. Coincidentally, they held residency at the same hospital in Los Angeles. At the time, as was a common practice among some medical residents, Zaetz and Katherine, both unmarried with no steady significant others, paired up as 'Fuck Buddies'.

Zaetz kept in touch with Katherine over the years, attended her wedding (to an anesthesiologist named Tom), and accepted the role of Godfather to her twin girls. Katherine was presently a Fellow at a prominent clinic in Chicago.

Picking her up at the airport for the medical seminar, Zaetz realized this was the first time they had been alone since their residency years. "I'm so glad you could come to the seminar, Kathy. I was surprised you were able to find the time."

Katherine smiled as Zaetz's Jaguar carried them

smoothly down the highway as if on feathers. "Well, the girls are in college now and I think Tom is occupied with some sweet, young, medical student," she explained. "And that's just as well. Gives me more free time."

"You don't seem upset. Is he serious about the girl?"

"Why Randy (Zaetz hadn't been called that in a while), I thought you knew. It's not a girl at all. Tom came out of the closet years ago."

They eyed each other and then laughed. Zaetz flipped on the turn signal. "Here's the hotel," he said as he directed the Jag into the Weston Oceanview Hotel's parking lot. "I reserved you a suite, so enjoy. Compliments of the hospital."

"If you have no other plans, Randy, why not join me for dinner. I'll just need a few minutes to shower and change out of my jet-lagged clothes. I always feel like I'm wearing wilted flowers after a flight." Katherine walked by Zaetz to the check-in desk with a porter carting her bags behind. "Unless you've got a sweet young thing waiting, that is."

Zaetz held up his hands. "Still a confirmed bachelor," he said with a smile. "And too old to be chasing youngsters anymore."

Zaetz accompanied Katherine to her suite, gave the porter a hefty tip, and surfed channels on the television while Katherine freshened up.

Katherine came out of the bathroom wet and wrapped in a towel. She had kept her figure. Her face was lustrous. Her thick head of auburn hair was wrapped turban–style inside a bath towel. She sat at the dressing table, removed the towel from her hair and let it fall damp and fragrant around her shoulders. In the mirror, she noticed Zaetz staring at her.

"Remember all the nights we spent on call at the hospital?" Katherine asked as she brushed her hair.

"How could I forget? Our fatigue was only eclipsed by our lust."

Katherine threw back her head and laughed. Zaetz stood up from the chair in front of the television and walked behind her.

"I haven't kept my figure like you have," Zaetz said as he rubbed his pot belly. "But I do try to maintain a decent exercise program." He positioned his hands on Katherine's shoulders; he bent down and placed a light kiss on each of them. As he did this, Zaetz gently moved the towel covering Katherine's shoulders away from her skin.

Katherine closed her eyes and said, "We could just order room service." But Zaetz had already slipped the towel completely free of her warm flesh by then.

***

"I seem to recall you had an interest in American Indian folklore," Zaetz remarked as his fingers lightly traced the spinal curve of Katherine's back; remains of lobster tails stared accusingly at him from the service cart by the bed.

Katherine stretched and turned over. She touched the tip of Zaetz's nose. "Hmmmm," she said with a mischievous grin. "What was it you asked?"

"Indian superstitions. Your thesis, right?"

"What an odd subject to bring up."

"It's a new patient of mine. Don't know if there really is any connection, but I recall you mentioned one tribe that worshiped a Great Mother who originated in the ocean."

"Let's see," Katherine mused; she propped herself on one elbow and playfully tousled Zaetz's thinning hair. "There was one group who worshipped a Great Mother that lived in the ocean. I see your memory is not affected by age yet either, Randy." She stopped twirling his hair and asked, "How do you think your patient is connected?"

"He dreams he is underwater. An exotic female figure is with him. They are not hampered by their surroundings, and they breathe as easily as if they had gills. Before she seduces him, the female figure whispers 'Mother.'"

"Ah ha! Oedipus stabs out his eyes yet again!"

Zaetz laughed. "That was my first thought, but the more I talked with him, the more my instinct tells me it's not the standard mother complex. Tell me more about your tribal study."

Katherine sat up and leaned against the headboard. Her small breasts danced as she slid back. Her nipples were still erect. "Well, I suppose their worship of the ocean goddess was much like a Mother Nature reference. The tribe was very big on the elementals: earth, wind, fire, and water. They believed these were feminine in nature and originated from the Great Mother in the ocean. All things were just tiny parts of a whole. The whole being the goddess." Katherine picked up the phone and dialed room service. "Hello, this is Dr. Phillips in 702. Could you send up an order of toast, coffee, and fruit for two? Thanks so much." She hung up and turned to Zaetz. "Come to think of it, the tribe buried their dead in the ocean."

"Really," Zaetz answered, unable to take his eyes off Katherine's breasts.

Katherine caught Zaetz ogling her. "Yes," she said and scooted across the bed and closer to Zaetz. "They believed the soul came from the Great Mother and should be given back." She lifted the covers and considered his erection. "I see you don't depend on Viagra," Katherine said as she seized him with one hand. "What a refreshing development these days."

As they made love for the second time, Zaetz offered a small prayer of thanks to his new patient Robert Adams and his story of the seduction under water that had given Zaetz's normally flaccid penis new life. Amen and hallelujah.

By the time Katherine and Zaetz finished, the toast and coffee sitting on a cart outside her suite had cooled.

***

Where are you, Robert?

Bobby, my dad calls me Bobby.

Where are you, Bobby?

On the pier. Dad took me fishing today.

Is your mother with you?

No, she said it was going to rain so she stayed home.

Is it raining?

No, it's just cold and cloudy.

What are you doing?

Looking at a mess of fish guts, they really stink.

Why do you look so worried, Bobby?

Dad's yelling at me.

Why?

He says I'm too close to the edge. He says something else but I can't... Help me! Help me, Dad!

What's wrong?

I'm slipping on the fish mess. I grab for the rail but miss. I'm falling.

Where are you?

I... I

Bobby?

It's cold and dark. My chest hurts. My nose burns. Bubbles tickle my face.

Can you open your eyes?

Yes, but it burns.

What do you see?

It's dark. I'm scared. I can't breathe... wait, there's someone else down here.

Who is it, Bobby?

A lady.

What does she look like?

A lady in the dark, but I can see her. She's waving at me. She wants me to come to her.

What does she want?

She's so cold. I'm shivering. She's kissing me; she's sucking out my air. My chest is on fire! Help! Help! Help!

Bobby?

…

Bobby?

Yes.

Where are you now?

Black.

Is the lady with you?

Black.

Is she with you in the water?

Nothing is here.

Bobby?

Bobby's not here.

Where is he?

He's free. He's with her.

The lady?

AAAAAUUUUUGGGGGHHHHH !!!!!

What's wrong?

Someone's grabbing me. Pressing on my chest hard. Hurts bad, real bad!

What?

No, stop it! I don't want to breathe. Want to stay with

her. Want to… I'M BACK! DAD, I'M BACK!

***

"Try to relax, Mr. Adams."

Adams was confused. Where the hell was he? "What's happening to me?" he asked as he tried to catch his breath.

Zaetz stood over Adams with a glass of water. "Take a drink of this," Zaetz instructed. "It's water with a mild sedative. The hypnosis was quite an ordeal for you."

Adams realized he was lying on the couch in Zaetz's office, and that he was soaked with sweat. He raised his head and took a small sip of the bitter liquid Zaetz offered.

Was I really hypnotized? Adams asked himself. The question swirled around his nausea and trembling muscles.

"I can't remember being under," Adams said. "Was I? Was I really?"

Zaetz took the glass from Adams and sat it down on the coffee table in front of the couch. There had been one moment during hypnosis that was critical. Adams' heart beat became irregular and racing, enough so to alert Zaetz to bring an immediate halt to the procedure. It seemed that Adams had recovered though, and that fact brought relief to Zaetz. The last thing he needed was a law suit from an irate wife over a husband's questionable death while under hypnosis.

"You don't remember anything?" Zaetz asked.

"No, nothing." Adams was relaxed now. His breathing and heart rate normal.

"That happens sometimes. What you experienced was

the memory of your near drowning. I feel it is appropriate to share what you said while under hypnosis in order to find an answer for your sleep disorder." Zaetz walked back to his desk. "As you agreed to in the consent forms, I taped the session. I strongly suggest this practice to all my patients who have opted for hypnosis because most of them, like you, don't remember what was revealed while they were under. If I merely told them what they said, there could always be a doubt as to my honesty. But this way," Zaetz continued while he held a finger above the play button on his portable cassette player, "there can be no suspicions. Shall I play your session for you, Mr. Adams?"

***

By the time the tape finished, Adams was sitting up and holding his face in his hands. "So I almost died that day."

"Clinically, you probably were dead. The pushing on your chest was surely CPR being performed. Many people who have drowned have been rescued from death just as you were, Mr. Adams."

"So this is the root of my problem: the water, the strange lady," Adams commented and lay back down. "But why now, after all these years?"

Zaetz lit his pipe. An aromatic, gray cloud permeated the room. "You repressed the incident, Mr. Adams. When you moved back here, the memory was triggered by some stimulus, probably the fact you are now living near the ocean. Your subconscious has been testing you, so to speak, seeing if you could bear the burden of remembering."

"Just doesn't seem to be the answer though. I think I could have handled the fact I survived. Seems like a positive thing to me."

Zaetz put down his pipe. "There is a logical explanation," he said, "something that is quite common among near death survivors."

"I'm all ears."

"Survivors subconsciously feel they have cheated death."

"Isn't that a good thing? Cheating death?"

"Not necessarily. At first they feel relieved, but over time their subconscious will remind them of their escape, especially in dream states. The patients I've helped complained they felt death was stalking them, returning to claim what was snatched away."

A visible shiver danced down Adam's spine.

"Of course, that scenario is impossible," Zaetz continued. "A rational mind will see this. But deep in our psyche all sorts of devils play with our thoughts. Superstitions, religious beliefs, and things we see or hear as children etch a permanent record in our brains. And death? Well, we hear about death all the time. We experience it first hand with relatives and friends. Death is so much a part of our daily lives as to seem animate. And being animate, there exists the delusion death is not just a state but also a living being who can come and seize what once belonged to it."

"So where does this leave me?" Adams asked. "Will I be able to sleep normally now that I know what happened the day I almost died? Will my subconscious be clear now?"

Zaetz smiled. "I think we made great progress today,

Mr. Adams. But it has been my experience in similar cases that continued therapy is the only assurance."

"How long?"

"That will depend entirely on you. I can say that since you were not plagued with this problem until you returned to a locale near your accident, the diagnosis is very favorable for a short recovery time."

"So I'll probably still have the dream?"

"I would be surprised if you didn't." Zaetz pulled out a prescription pad from his desk. "I would like to start you on some medication, Mr. Adams. Something to help you sleep."

Adams stood and shook his head no. "Don't bother. I've been given so many different pills my medicine cabinet 'overfloweth.'"

"Have you ever taken Desyrel?"

"Doesn't ring a bell, but, like I said, there's been so many."

Zaetz rummaged in his desk drawers and then came away with a blister pack. "Tell you what, here's a seven day sample pack of Desyrel. Check your other scripts when you get home. If you haven't been given Desyrel, try it for a few nights. If it helps, give me a call and I'll fax a month's prescription to your drug store."

Adams took the blister pack. Looking through the raised bubbles, he saw green and white capsules lined up like sentries ready for duty. "What exactly will this do for me?"

"It should allow you to sleep through the night. It's a common therapy for patients who have sleep disturbances from a Melatonin hormone imbalance. They suffer 'jet-lag' symptoms without actually flying."

"But that doesn't sound like my problem."

"No, but it will keep you from waking up in the middle of a dream and allow you continued sleep for a while after."

"So it won't stop the dream?"

"Only the abrupt waking from."

Adams sighed. "Well, I suppose anything's worth a try, as long as I haven't already taken it I mean."

"Be sure and check with my secretary on the way out, Mr. Adams. She will set you up for our next appointment," Zaetz said as he stood up and walked to the office door. Opening the door for Adams, Zaetz added, "And don't forget to let me know if the drug is helpful so I can fax that prescription for you."

Adams held out his hand. "Thanks, Doc. I appreciate your help."

"Your quite welcome, Mr. Adams," Zaetz said and shook Adams' hand. "By the way, Mr. Adams, do have any native Indian ancestry?"

Adams released the handshake. "As a matter of fact, my mother used to mention my grandmother was part Indian. Why do you ask?"

"Just curious. You have high cheek bones. A trait of American Tribes."

Adams smiled. "Guess Mom was right then. See you next week, Doc."

As he closed the door and walked to his desk and sat down, Zaetz thought about Katherine's information on Indian legends and considered that a young Robert Adams may have heard about a Great Mother living in the ocean from his grandmother. That memory, stored with millions of other bits of information, could well have surfaced in a brain starved of oxygen. A brain that saw and felt a dark lady under the water as it drowned.

***

Sandra Adams informed her sister that Robert seemed to feel good about his therapy. "He called and said the doctor had some interesting ideas," Sandra voiced as she dumped a steaming tangle of pasta into a strainer over the sink. Her sister's small apartment was a palette of warm, starchy tang laced with the sharp aroma of bubbling marinara sauce. "He's given Robert a new sleeping pill to try," Sandra continued as her sister, June, dark haired and stocky compared to Sandra's blonde, thin frame, came into the kitchen holding a bottle of Merlot.

"You're crazy to have left Robert over a silly dream," June said as she removed a corkscrew from a cabinet drawer and twisted the metal into the wine bottle's cork. "As unlucky with men as I've been, I wouldn't care if he was humping the Rockette Chorus Line in his sleep as long as he stuck around the next morning."

Sandra laughed and started to set the kitchen table. "Maybe you're right, Sis. I just overreacted, but I think me moving out made Robert try to get help sooner than he would have." Sandra wiped her hands on an apron and added with a sigh, "I do miss him though. I don't see any harm in going back tomorrow. Do you, Sis?"

"Why not tonight?" June asked and filled Sandra's glass with the dark, red, passion of heaven.

"Robert told me he needs to try out that new pill by himself. I'll call him in the morning to see if it helped." Sandra lifted the wine glass to her lips and took a sip. Her cheeks flushed and the food on the table suddenly smelled gorgeous. "Besides," Sandra remarked, "after supper aren't we suppose to cheer for that young stud on *American Idol*?"

***

Robert Adams pondered on his conversation with Sandra earlier on the phone that evening. She seemed supportive again, like she had stopped worrying about Robert's dream woman.

Holding one of the green and white capsules in his hand, Adams said out loud, "Here's hope for a good night's sleep and that my wife comes home tomorrow like she promised." Adams then slipped the capsule in his mouth, took a drink of water, stripped, turned off the light, lay on the fresh sheets he had placed around the mattress minutes before, and waited.

Eventually, sleep slid over Adams like a warm buzz. His body relaxed and the dream arrived as it always did: his boyhood room, the moon glowing full through the ripples of a world under water, the silhouette of the woman and her movements as she approaches his naked body. "Mother," she whispered again and held Robert's erection and then positioned him inside her. But this time, Robert did not awaken. Zaetz's prediction of the drug's effectiveness held true.

The woman moved slowly on top of him, pacing her

desire. Robert was deep inside her but could not move. She controlled every motion as she approached climax, and Robert didn't care if she did. He had never felt this kind of sensation before. It was beyond pleasure. He felt as if his body would suddenly tear apart in the agony of an intense orgasm.

The woman threw back her head and opened her eyes wide. They possessed no pupils. They were solid obsidian and glinted in the moonlight. As the woman climaxed, so did Robert. His release of pressure inside her was a relief and an ecstasy. And as he filled her, Robert opened his mouth to cry out and water rushed into his lungs.

***

Zaetz had drifted into sleep thinking about Adams and wondered if the drug he prescribed would be of any help to the haggard man. He was awakened by the phone. Checking the clock radio on his nightstand, Zaetz's blurred vision came to focus on the fact it was four a.m. He reached for the receiver, knocked it off the hook and then reached down and clumsily felt around the carpet to retrieve it.

"Yes?" Zaetz said still half asleep." Yes?"

"Dr. Randolph Zaetz?"

His head a bit clearer, Zaetz answered, "Yes."

"So sorry to disturb you at this early hour, Dr. Zaetz. My name is Broders, Detective Broders, Homicide Division San Diego PD."

Zaetz's drowsiness evaporated. "Homicide? What on earth?"

"There's been an incident involving a patient of yours.

124

Is Robert Adams still under your care? We found your name on a business card in his wallet."

Zaetz rubbed his eyes. What in the world could have happened? "Yes, I saw him yesterday afternoon and on one previous occasion. Is he all right?" Zaetz chided himself after the question. Homicide? Sure he's all right. Nothing wrong here.

"I'm afraid Mr. Adams is deceased."

"Oh, no," Zaetz said in a whisper. "What happened?"

Broders paused before asking, "Would it be too inconvenient for you to come to Adam's house, Dr. Zaetz? You might be able to help answer some questions while the crime scene is still fresh."

"Perhaps I could aid you on the phone."

"No, you'll understand when you get here. But if you'd rather not come now, we can interview you down at headquarters later."

Zaetz was certain this detective thought that he was involved somehow. He thought he might as well go and clear up any idea of such a crazy notion. "No, I'll come now. You'll have to give me his address. I don't keep any of my patient's records at home because of privacy issues."

Zaetz was headed down the highway within fifteen minutes of ending the phone conversation with Broders. A quick sponge bath, tooth brushing and casual dress of jeans, tee shirt and gray hoody had him out the door quickly with a thermal cup of coffee grasped tightly in his hands to take off the morning chill from the ocean air.

Adams' house was surprisingly near Zaetz's own. Clear Bluff Street was only about ten miles away. It was really not a street at all though. A line of frame condos snaked down the beach about a hundred yards from the water. It wasn't hard for Zaetz to guess where Adams' residence was. Six cars—two police cruisers, and four unmarked law enforcement vehicles—fanned out in front of it.

Sunrise was still a good two hours away when Zaetz got out of his car and walked to the front door of Adams' condo. A uniformed officer asked Zaetz what his business there was and then directed him into the house where he asked Zaetz to wait in a short hallway.

As he waited, Zaetz observed the state of Adams' home. It was a small place. The hall routed itself to three doors. The one nearest Zaetz was opened and led into a living room-kitchen combination: tiny kitchen, small living room with a leather sofa, coffee table, end table, and a high def television mounted on the wall. And everything was undisturbed. No evidence of foul play in this room, Zaetz thought.

The next door, a little farther down the hall, was slightly ajar. Zaetz couldn't see in completely, but a reflection of the shower in a mirror inferred it to be the bathroom.

It was out of the third door a fiftyish, short, slumped, balding man appeared. He walked down the hall and extended his hand to Zaetz.

"I'm Detective Broders," the man said. "Thank you for coming down on such short notice at this ungodly hour."

Zaetz released the detective's hand. "Always glad to be of help," Zaetz said. "What can I do?"

"Please accompany me to the bedroom and have a look at the body."

Zaetz followed Broders into the last doorway, the bedroom. Like the living room and kitchen, it seemed intact. The dresser opposite the bed was in place. Small items on it like a hairbrush, perfume bottles, and a jewelry box implied a woman's presence, but they too were secure and unmolested. The only hint of disorder was the nude, spread-eagled body of Robert Adams lying in the center of a queen size bed.

Adams' face was frozen; his eyes bulged. His appearance mimicked that of a person coming into a darkened room only to be stunned by friends gathered for a surprise birthday party.

"What do you think of the bed?" Broders asked and pointed at the water-logged bed that looked as if a tidal wave had slammed into it.

Zaetz couldn't believe what he saw and could only shrug his shoulders.

"Or this," Broders said and stood above the body. The police photographer along with other investigators scrutinizing the area moved away from the bed as Broders put a hand on Adams' chest and gave a strong push. A spout of water shot from Adams' mouth and nose.

Zaetz jumped back like someone had goosed him. "But how is that possible?"

"I have no clue. How do you think a man can drown in his bed, Dr. Zaetz?"

Zaetz was astonished. "That's physically impossible. It cannot happen unless he was drowned somewhere else then put back in his bed."

"That occurred to me. It was his wife, after all, who called us about him."

"His wife?"

"Oddest thing. She phoned in around two this morning. Said she had a terrible premonition something had happened to her husband. She wouldn't stop talking until she was assured it would be checked out."

"Do you think she did this? I know from my sessions with her husband that she was upset with him. He said she had moved in with her sister."

"That possibility also occurred to me, but I don't see it." Broders ran his hand across the bed and then walked over to Zaetz. He held his finger under Zaetz's nose and Zaetz pulled away. "That's salt water," Broders remarked. "I doubt she drowned him in the ocean and was able to bring him back here without any drag marks or evidence of sand anywhere in this house."

Zaetz felt he was now, for whatever reason, being interrogated as a possible suspect. "I can tell you Mr. Adams was my patient, Detective, but the specifics of his case, as you are aware, remain privileged."

Broders smiled. "That may well be, Dr. Zaetz, but if our investigation turns up no other clues, we can, as you are aware, get that information."

Zaetz relented. "What is it that you want to know, Detective?"

"Among other things, what could cause that?" Broders

said and pointed toward Adams' corpse.

In the shock and confusion of being summoned here at so early an hour and the tragic circumstances involved, Zaetz had failed to notice the towering erection that rose from Adams. It was huge, pale, and awesome.

"He didn't hang himself," Broders continued, "so why the boner?"

Zaetz shook his head. The fact of the administered drug Desyrel then popped into his befuddled brain. "It's priapism," Zaetz said.

"What?"

"I recently prescribed a sleep medication for Mr. Adams. One of the side effects can be an extended erection known as priapism. Sometimes the only way to relieve it is to surgically cut the penile shaft open and drain out the blood."

A look of dismay spread over Broders' face. Unconsciously he reached down and covered his crotch. "Could he have accidentally overdosed?" he asked.

"It's possible. But for a side effect to occur that quickly something out of the ordinary had to have happened. If alcohol was involved, that could very well explain it. Of course, not the drowning part."

Broders put his hands on his hips. "God, I hate these weird-ass cases," he said with exhaustion "Well, I suppose we'll take him down to the coroner for an autopsy. That's all I can think to ask you tonight, Dr. Zaetz, but I'll probably need you to come down later this week, so stick around town."

"Just give me a call, Detective."

Broders shook his head and said, "Christ, I almost forgot. I still have to tell his wife. Shit, sometimes I really hate this job."

As Zaetz turned away, he was startled by a tearing sound behind him. He turned around and discovered it was the zipper on a body bag being dragged up and over Adams' erection, which prodded through the plastic like a finger pointing to heaven.

Zaetz walked out of the room, down the hall and then out through the front door. The skyline was still empty of any breath of morning.

As he got in his car, Zaetz reached for the half-full thermal coffee container. "Whoever invented this is a genius," he said as he tilted the cup and took a long swallow of the hot liquid; he needed to feel the reality of its burning all the way down to the pit of his stomach to clear away the lunacy of the dead man's condition he had just witnessed.

***

The rush of the encroaching morning began to settle in Zaetz's head; the cobwebs converged into straight lines. All the aspects of Adams' dream bore down on his conscious mind like a roaring locomotive. He started his car and drove further down the beach until the long line of condos had vanished and there was nothing but the sand and the waves. There, numerous jetties extended into the ocean like black fingers. He pulled close to one and cut off the car's engine.

Zaetz got out and sat on the warm hood of the car. "A dream cannot materialize," he told himself. "A dream could kill if one suffered from cardiovascular difficulties, but it could not physically manifest itself."

130

So how did Adams die then? Zaetz looked at the dark waters before him. A breeze came in off the ocean. He shivered as it flowed over him. He slid off the car hood and walked toward the shoreline. He began stripping, first his hoody and tee shirt, then his jeans, boxers, tennis shoes, and socks. The wind slapped him with its chill. Coming to the jetty, Zaetz strode into the water by its side. In a few moments, he was chest deep in the cold water. The waves were gentle but still splashed and sent frigid, salty kisses to his face and lips. Zaetz then dove under and immersed himself. His muscles constricted; his diaphragm was paralyzed for an instant by the shock of the cold. His penis shriveled. His testicles retracted and left an empty scrotal sac behind.

Zaetz surfaced. His body began to adjust, and he started swimming further out in long graceful strokes.

After an eternity of minutes, Zaetz stopped swimming and dog-paddled in one spot. The gloomy vastness of water expanded infinitely before him. Adams's exhausted face emerged in his mind.

"You'll have to prove it to me," Zaetz said in a whisper.

Zaetz took a long, deep breath and then went under the water. Below, all was darkness until a certain, dim and distant illumination crossed his vision.

Zaetz expelled the burden of air in his lungs and drifted downward until he rested on the coarse, sandy bottom.

There, the shadows dissipated frostily around him.

There, a shadow within those shadows, Zaetz patiently awaited *her* embrace.

Rain, Rain, Go Away! *Please...*

Vincent Bivona

Simon stared at the tiny red berries through the lenses of his glasses. "What are you talking about? They're poisonous! You can't eat those!"

"Yeah, you can," Larry insisted. He puffed out his chest and squared his shoulders, making them seem almost as wide as when he had his football gear on. "I've seen my uncle do it once."

"Your uncle probably ate Wild Rose berries. These are *Yew*. Look at the seed, that's how you can tell the difference. It's visible from the outside and extremely toxic, one of the most deadly plant materials. Other than that, the berries look almost identical. If you want to eat these, fine, be my guest, but it's your funeral."

Larry stared at the berries in his hand for what felt like a long time. For a moment, Simon thought he was going to squish them in anger. At last, he hesitantly let them drop to the ground.

"Moron."

Simon whispered it a little too loudly because Jessica

shot him a reproachful look. She had invited him along to go hiking with her and her new boyfriend, hoping that the time together would force the two boys to like one another. By the way things were working out, it looked like it was going to be a complete disaster instead. They did nothing but bicker, trying to outdo the other.

"You know, you should really start working out," Larry said to Simon. "Put some meat on those bones. If your legs weren't so skinny, you wouldn't have such a hard time trying to make it up this incline."

"I can make it up just as easily as you can," Simon said, panting for breath.

Larry turned around, now walking backwards. "Oh, can you?" He hooked a thumb over his shoulder. "Tell you what then—first one to that rock up there wins. Loser pays for the park admission."

Jessica, seeing how tired Simon was, tried to put a stop to this before it even started. "Larry, maybe you guys shouldn't. I like walking, and if you guys run, we can't really look at all the leaves on the—"

But Simon cut her off before she even had a chance to finish. "You're on!"

The next thing she knew, the two boys were off, sprinting to the rock, Simon trailing long behind. Yeah, maybe trying to get the two of them to become friends wasn't such a good idea after all. It was like trying to make magnets with the same charges attract, except there was nothing similar about Larry and Simon. Larry was the starting quarterback on the school football team—attractive, muscular, popular—and Simon was… well, he was just Simon. He and

Jessica lived next door to each other and had grown up together. He was tall, skinny, wore glasses, had a rock collection, and built models. He wasn't like the average guy, and that was why he was the perfect best friend. He always called with interesting things to talk about and always cheered Jessica up when she was upset, knowing just what to say. The only thing they disagreed on were the types of guys Jessica dated, which always turned out to be douchebags who broke her heart. Jessica was hoping that Larry would be the exception to the rule, but it was obvious that Simon didn't seem to think so.

"I win!" Larry shouted from the top of the hill. He leaped onto the rock and pumped his fist into the air. "Victory!"

"You cheated," Simon gasped. He was doubled over with his hands on his knees, sucking in air. "You had a head start."

"Trust me; it wouldn't have made a difference. When it comes to a physical competition, I *always* win."

As if to show Simon how much he won, he wrapped his arm around Jessica's shoulder when she caught up to them. Simon watched the two of them walk ahead while he struggled behind, fighting to catch his breath. The sight of this upset him more than anything. It was like a dagger being slowly twisted into his heart. He'd had a crush on Jessica for as far back as he could remember, but he'd always been too afraid to tell her. He had initially hoped that she'd realize they would be perfect for each other. But by the way things panned out, it seemed that she tended to be attracted to jerks instead. It wasn't fair at all. He knew everything about her: her ambitions, her secrets, what upset her, what didn't. If there was anyone who should be dating her, it was him.

As if sensing what Simon was thinking, Larry looked back over his shoulder and flashed a mocking smile, showcasing a set of dazzlingly white teeth.

"Jerk!" Simon muttered under his breath, this time making sure Jessica couldn't hear him.

***

Thunder boomed in the distance, its gentle rumble shaking the ground. They were on the homestretch of the trail already. They had started an hour or two after sunup and had pushed on since then. Simon looked at the blue blazer nailed to one of the trees and checked their progress on the map. Thank God they were only about a quarter mile from the parking lot. Unlike a regular trail through the woods, this one had obstacles: steep inclines, fallen trees you had to duck under, rock scrambles you had to ascend, and rickety wooden ladders you had to climb. Jessica and Larry looked like they were having the time of their lives. Simon would have his when they were back at the car, where he could finally sit down.

"Look, a cave!" Jessica pointed out.

Sure enough, up ahead was a craggy set of rocks with an opening. Since they were already at the top of the formation, it only made sense that they would have to descend into the cave to continue along the trail. Peering in, it looked to be about twenty-five feet long, pitched at a steep diagonal, littered with sticks and twigs. Nothing too bad. But nothing Simon wanted to do either. He hoped it was the last obstacle. At least it would be shady in there—his fair skin needed a break from the intense beating sun.

"I'll send you guys a postcard from the bottom!" Larry shouted, and practically jumped down into the opening.

Jessica shot him a playful scowl. "Not if I get there first!"

Simon took his time, carefully placing one foot behind the other as he descended. He had just cleared the opening when the first drops of rain started to fall. Needing a break, he chanced a look down at the others. As usually, Larry was making the best progress. He was nearly at the bottom, moving from rock to rock with the ease of a mountain goat, his muscles rippling. It didn't even look like he was breathing heavily.

Jessica was a different story. It was as if somebody had switched her with another person. Unlike a few minutes ago, she looked pale and drawn and her face had broken out into ferocious beads of sweat. Simon had seen a sudden change like this come over her once or twice before and feared what it might imply.

"Jessica! Are you all right?"

She either ignored him or didn't hear. She continued her climb down into the cave, struggling to find foot- and handholds, moving slowly and sluggishly like she was trapped underwater.

"Jessica!"

This time she *did* look up. But when she did, Simon knew she was in trouble. Her eyes were barely open, and her head rocked from side to side as if she were dizzy. She opened her mouth to say something but never got it out. Instead, she lost her grip and fell down into the cave, Simon screaming after her.

Larry had already made it to the bottom. He was standing under the overhang, looking out into the drizzle, when he heard Simon scream.

"What happened?" he shouted. He snapped his head around at once to find his girlfriend lying sprawled out on the rocks. "Oh shit! Jessica! Jessica!" He scrambled over to her, inspecting her wounds. Thank God she had not been impaled by the sticks and twigs. "What the hell did you do?" he shouted at Simon.

Simon opened his eyes so wide in surprise that they nearly filled the lenses of his glasses. "*Me?* What the hell are you talking about? She fell! I didn't do anything!"

"Whatever!" Larry shoved his arms under her, preparing to lift her up.

"Don't move her! Are you stupid? She could have a spinal injury!"

"Don't tell me what to do. She's my girlfriend!"

"And she's *my* best friend! It's my job to look after her! I'm not letting you move her!"

Outside the rain suddenly picked up, slamming on the rocks that made up the cave, turning the inside into an echoing drum. It was beating so loudly that they almost didn't hear Jessica moan. She was staring into space, blinking, her hands slowly making their way to her ankle. It was the first time either of the boys noticed it. It was large and puffy, already beginning to swell.

"Shit, it's broken," Larry said at once.

"You don't know that," Simon countered. "It could just be a really bad sprain."

"Bobby Dulac broke his ankle at practice two weeks ago, and it looked just like that. It's broken."

Simon felt like his head was going to explode. "It doesn't matter, okay? She's hurt. She needs medical attention right away."

"Then let's get her some." He bent to pick her up.

Without thinking, Simon punched Larry in the shoulder. "Are you stupid? Were you even listening to me before?"

Larry whirled around, shoving a finger in Simon's face. "If you ever hit me again—*ever!*—it'll be the last thing you ever do. Understand?"

Simon swallowed hard. He opened his mouth to respond, when he caught a whiff of something odd.

Larry said, "Hey, I'm talking to you. Answer me."

"Do you smell that?" Simon asked instead.

"Don't try to change the subject. We need to get a few things straight here, you and me. You're—"

"No, I'm serious. I smell something." The concern in his voice was unmistakable. He stuck his nose into the air and sniffed the way a dog does that has caught a scent. "It almost smells like... like sulfuric acid."

"Sulfuric what?"

"Sulfuric acid. It's a highly corrosive liquid. You know, it eats away at things."

"You're crazy," Larry said. "There's nothing out here like that."

It was then that Simon noticed the smoke near the opening at the bottom of the cave. At first it looked like little tendrils of fog coming off the ground. But when he crept down to look out into the wilderness, he could see that it was rising off the plants and vegetation. Like they were *burning*.

He was about to say something when there was a loud *Thump!* as something struck the ground a few feet away from him. To his surprise, it was a bird. A large blue jay that had fallen right out of the sky. The disconcerting part was that the bird was smoldering, smoke rising from its charred body. It looked like someone had taken a lighter to it, the bird's feathers half-melted like Icarus's wings. The horror didn't stop there. Its eyes were filmy and cloudy, and its beak was disintegrating right before Simon's very eyes.

"What the hell happened to that thing?" Larry asked from behind.

Before Simon could answer, there was another *Thump!* and then another. All around him birds whistled down from the sky like hail, crashing into trees, falling from the heavens and plummeting down to earth. Each of them smoldering like a half-cooked chicken.

"Sulfuric acid…" Simon said slowly, his voice barely above a whisper.

"What?"

He turned to Larry. "Sulfuric acid. It's in the rain. It's killing them."

"Wait, you mean, like, it's raining *acid?*"

He looked back out at the charred carcasses. "That's exactly what I mean."

Larry shook his head, refusing to believe this. "That's ridiculous! It can't rain acid!"

"Well it can, and it is! And it's killing whatever's unfortunate enough to have gotten stuck out there in it!"

At the sound of their shouting, Jessica moaned. Larry climbed back over to her and grabbed her hand, hoping to calm her. To Simon, he said, "If that's the case, then thank God she broke her ankle in here, where there's a roof over our heads."

That ignited Simon's fuse. "What the hell's wrong with you? It would have been better if she hadn't broken her ankle at all! Do you know how much trouble we're in?"

"Not as much as you're making it out to be, that's for sure. It's bad, but it's only her ankle. We'll wait till the rain stops, and then we can get—"

"It's *not* only her ankle! She's going into seizure."

As if on cue, Jessica started to shake, her limbs twitching and convulsing violently, her eyes rolling around in her head.

"Oh God!" Larry shouted. "What's wrong with her? Why's she shaking?"

"You don't know anything about her, do you?" Simon snapped. "She's diabetic."

"Shit! What do we do?"

"We need to test her blood sugar. Quick, open her

backpack. There should be a little black box inside. Give it to me."

Larry did as he was told, and Simon tested her blood.

He sucked in air through his teeth when he saw the numbers, and then cursed a second later. "This isn't good."

"What?"

"It's really low. She needs a glucose injection, and it isn't in here."

"Where is it?" Larry asked, worry written all over his face.

"I don't know," said Simon. "But she has extras in her car. In her glove box." He thought for a second. "Do you have anything sugary on you?"

Larry shook his head.

"Damn!"

"Is she gonna be okay?" Larry asked.

"No, without her glucose, she's either going to slip into a coma or die."

"Die?"

"Yes, die."

"How the hell are we gonna get it with *that* going on?" He pointed out the opening at the bottom of the cave and into the forest. The rain had turned into a torrential downpour, beating a maddening tattoo on the rocks. It didn't show any sign of letting up. In the distance lightning, almost supernaturally bright, painted the sky, and thunder roared, quaking the earth.

"I don't know," Simon said at last. "I just don't know."

***

At first the rocks they were sitting on were dry, but after a time, the acid rain pouring into the opening at the top of the cave finally trickled down the diagonal tube, wetting them. Larry noticed this when he put his hand out and felt his skin sizzling.

"This is ridiculous," he said after hissing in pain and wiping his hand on his shirt. "We can't stay here." He'd been sitting with Jessica, rubbing her trembling body. Now he stood up, crept to the bottom of the cave, where a small puddle of acid was forming, and peered out into the poisonous waterfall that had become the earth.

"Well, then what do you suppose we do?" Simon asked.

Larry grabbed the map from his pocket. "This says we're only about a quarter mile from the parking lot. I could sprint back to the car and get her that shot."

Simon looked at him doubtfully. "In the rain?"

"I run a six-minute mile. I'll only be out in it for a second or two."

"Try a minute and a half."

Larry gave him a hard stare. "Do you have any better ideas? You said it yourself: If she doesn't get that shot, she'll die. We have to do something. We can't just sit around, waiting for the rain to stop."

"You're the one who wanted to sit around in the first place," Simon pointed out.

"That was before I knew she was diabetic and she went into a seizure! Christ, why are you arguing with me?"

Simon didn't know. He supposed it was because he hated himself for not being the one volunteering to put his life on the line for Jessica's. He would have done it, easily, no hesitation, if there was a chance of succeeding. But he knew with his poor stamina that he'd never make it back, and he doubted killing himself would be of any help to her.

"Gimme her keys," Larry said.

While Simon fished them out of her backpack, Larry pulled off the tank top he wore under his shirt and wrapped it around his head. When he was finished, he looked Middle Eastern, with only a slit in the fabric for his eyes to peer through.

"Smart," said Simon, handing him the keys.

"I'll be back as soon as I can."

With one final look at Jessica, Larry sprinted out into the pelting rain.

Simon watched as it saturated his clothes. And then he watched as the smoke started to rise off them.

***

"Hang in there," Simon told Jessica. He'd been sitting with her for what felt like fifteen minutes, doing nothing but peering out into the downpour. It had started to rain even harder, if that was possible. Large buckets of acid surged down from the sky as if there was a giant pool up there that had sprung a leak. The virulent liquid saturated the earth, searing whatever life it came in contact with, creating small bowls of bubbling fluid in the mud. Something about the situation gnawed at Simon's mind, but he couldn't quite put his finger on it. Worrying about the rain easily took over his thoughts. The tiny trickle from the opening above had now become a small stream. It slued into their tiny shelter, blanketing the rocks. Already the small puddle at the bottom of the cave had become a small pond, the water level rising. Simon knew it was only a matter of time before it got too high to escape. Already he would have to submerge his foot up to his ankle if he stepped into it.

Where the hell was Larry? By Simon's calculations, he should have been back by now. Simon didn't think he could wait any longer. Not by the way the water level was rising, and not with the way Jessica looked. The color of her skin had paled considerably, and it was damp and clammy to the touch. She had stopped trembling as much, but Simon took that as a bad sign. That meant she was closer to slipping into a coma. She needed that glucose injection.

Simon knew he didn't come anywhere close in strength to Larry and therefore couldn't carry Jessica back to the car, but maybe he could devise something to drag her with. He frantically scoured the cave, his mind working feverishly. He happened upon the sticks and twigs and figured they were the best he was going to come up with. It would have been better if they were longer, but beggars couldn't be choosers. He arranged them in the shape of a rectangle with two ends jutting out for handles. It was easy, just like building one of his models, only this one was much larger. Next, he pulled off his undershirt and began ripping it into little strips, which he used to tie the ends of the sticks together. He wrapped the remainder of the fabric around his head, like Larry. When he was done he had a head wrap and a crudely constructed travois, a frame on which he could place Jessica and pull her.

Getting her onto it didn't present a problem. What did was the fact that her face would be exposed to the rain the moment he pulled her out of the cave. Cursing with himself for not having considered this, he did the only thing he could think of: He pulled the very shirt off his back and used it to fashion *her* a head wrap. The rain was going to burn his bare skin like hell, but she was worth it.

***

Sure enough it was like nothing he had ever felt before, like thousands of sharp, serrated knives gnawing at his upper torso. He cried out at first, unable to help himself. Then he gritted his teeth when he realized he was only wasting his breath. If there was one good thing to say about the incredible pain, it was that it made him run faster than he thought was possible. Now he knew how a horse felt when a jockey whipped it with his crop.

He sprinted over the wet ground, doing his best to avoid splashing in puddles. He stumbled a number of times. At one point he tripped and fell face-first into the mud, coating his head wrap in the corrosive goo. Fearing that it would eat through the fabric and then begin to consume the skin on his face, he frantically tore it off and tossed it away. Now he had no protection against the elements at all.

Jessica wasn't that far off. Her head wrap had begun to smoke. Enough so that Simon had to pull her under a large tree and remove the fabric covering her skin. He was just in time, too, because it had almost soaked all the way through.

Simon wondered how far they were from the car. He looked around, trying to get his bearings, when he noticed Larry pressed up against an outcropping of rock about eighty feet to his left, using the overhang as an awning. He, too, had pulled off his headgear. At the sight of him, Simon felt a surge of relief. And for the first time he was surprised to find that he was actually happy to see one of Jessica's boyfriends.

"Thank God," Simon yelled over to him. "Did you get the—"

He never got to finish his sentence. It was only then that he noticed the animal standing in front of Larry, cornering him. The thing had been out in the elements for so long that it barely had any distinguishing features left. What had once been a shiny gray pelt was now a scorched ruin of blistering pink skin. Deformed ears sagged on its head, barely clinging on by threads of charred flesh. A long snout jutted from its face, eaten through, exposing the collapsed tunnels of its nasal cavity. Like the birds that had fallen out of the sky, both of the wolf's eyes were blind, milky white ruins. Yet, despite its lack of vision, it seemed to know exactly where it was going.

At the sound of Simon's voice, it snapped its head around. Then, in an all-out sprint, it charged straight at Simon, letting loose a vicious, lamenting growl.

Caught off guard, Simon did the only thing he could do—he shot out his arms in a warding-off gesture and accepted the wolf in a hugging embrace. One second it was in the air, the next it was on him, sinking its teeth into his forearm. If he had thought the acid against his bare skin hurt, then this was beyond description. He yowled in pain, trying to wrench his arm free. It was no use. It was as if he had gotten it stuck in a vice made out of nails.

Not knowing what else to do, he balled his free hand into a fist and beat the wolf's face in an attempt to make it let go. To his surprise, it did. It growled, snapping at the fist attacking it. Simon pulled his hand away just in time, the wolf's razor-sharp teeth closing on the space it had occupied only a second before. Then it lunged, preparing to bite again.

That's when Simon kicked out as hard as he could. His sneaker connected with the wolf's grotesque, deteriorating face, throwing the animal sideways. The impact was so sudden that it knocked Simon over, too, sprawling him backwards. There was a sudden, blinding pain as the top of his head splashed into a puddle. He yanked it out and backed under the tree, slapping at his wet hair. He thought he was going to go mad from the pain. That's when he realized the wolf already had. It was on the ground now, floundering like a fish that had been jerked out of water. It was beyond the point of standing up. By the way it looked, it had broken one of its legs when it tumbled over. Now, it just lay there, shuddering, as the acid chased its life away.

That's when Simon realized he and Jessica couldn't wait around any longer. The rain had already eaten through their headgear. It was only a matter of time before it consumed everything else.

"Did you get the shot?" Simon called over to Larry. His legs felt like Jell-O, and he had to shoot out a hand and clutch the trunk of the tree to keep from falling.

"Nice to see you, too," Larry shouted back. "By the way, thanks for taking care of the wolf. Guess you're good for something, after all."

Simon pretended he hadn't heard this, his anger rising. "Did you get the shot or not?"

Larry shook his head. When he spotted Jessica lying on the travois, he wrapped his arms over his face and darted over under the tree, hissing in pain as the rain sizzled his skin.

"Is she okay?"

"No," Simon said. "She's worse than ever. We need that shot."

Larry pointed past the rock outcropping. "The car's not that far. Maybe a hundred yards that way. I saw it, but then that *thing* tried to eat me."

That was all Simon needed to hear. "Then we have to go." He lifted the travois, his arms trembling.

Larry noticed. "Are you sure she's not too heavy for you?"

Simon remembered how he'd stumbled and tripped. And that was *before* the encounter with the wolf. Escaping so narrowly had sapped the strength out of him. "No," he admitted. "I mean, she is too heavy. I don't know if I can carry her back without falling."

"Then here, let me take her."

Simon tightened his grip, refusing to let go.

"Come on," Larry insisted. "You already saved my life, at least let me save hers. You can make it to the car if you didn't have to pull her, right?"

Simon nodded. He thought he could at least manage that.

"Okay, then let me take her."

At last Simon let go, letting Larry step into the travois.

***

The car sat in the middle of the parking lot, alone and forlorn. The acid rain had already eaten through the tires, forcing it to sag into the ground. It looked abandoned, a landmark from an alien time, but seeing it still raised the boys' spirits.

Even with the additional weight, Larry beat Simon to the vehicle. This was a good thing, because it meant that Jessica didn't have to spend as much time in the rain.

Before they had set out on this last leg of their journey, Larry had copied Simon's actions and pulled off his shirt, draping it over Jessica's head for protection against the biting rain. Now having reached the car, his back scorched and beginning to blister, he let go of the travois and plunged his hands into his pockets.

The keys weren't there.

That was it. All hope was lost. Then he remembered he'd stuck them in his back pocket and fished them out.

"Help me lift her!" he shouted when he got the car door open. "And whatever you do, don't drop her!"

Simon grabbed the back end of the travois and lifted.

"Not a chance!" he shouted back as he helped Jessica in.

Even though his eyes were practically squinted closed against the rain, he could see the concern on Larry's face. Maybe he'd been wrong about him, after all. Maybe this guy *did* care.

Simon found out just how much Larry cared when the

two of them climbed into the car. Larry didn't pause in the slightest; he tore the glove compartment open, nearly ripping it off its hinges, and rooted around for the glucose injection.

"Found it!" Larry cried. He held out the needle like it was a trophy he'd just won.

"Great. Give it to me!" Simon shouted.

He thought Larry might argue, but he didn't. He handed it over easily, watching with concern as Simon rolled up Jessica's sleeve and injected her with the life-saving formula. He hadn't noticed at first, but being out of the acid rain was absolute bliss. It pounded on the windshield and thrummed on the sheet metal of the car, but for what it was worth, it couldn't get in. That was okay by him. What was more than okay was the fact that Jessica was starting to come around. She had stopped shaking and was beginning to open her eyes.

"You all right?" Simon asked her.

She mumbled something incomprehensible. He thought it was along the lines of *I will be.*

"Is she gonna be all right?" Larry echoed.

Simon let out a huge sigh of relief. "She's gonna be—" *fine* was how he intended to finish. But at that moment he looked out the windshield and into the sky beyond. In the distance, far off on the horizon, was the blackest cloud he had ever seen. A dark, cancerous mass rising out of the ground like an open umbrella.

All the time he'd been trapped in the cave with Jessica while it rained, something had been gnawing at his mind. Now, it hit him. It had been the sky. It had been a clear blue.

Staring at that great big mushroom cloud in the distance, Simon understood why the sun had been out while it had been thundering. It had never been thunder at all. It had been the nukes detonating. The ones the foreign powers must have dropped. He remembered that sulfuric acid was used in the construction of certain kinds of explosives and finally understood what the super-bright lightning and acid rain implied. He didn't think they were going to be all right after all. In fact, that was the farthest thing from what they were going to be. All at once, everything trivial ceased to matter. It didn't matter who liked Jessica more—him or Larry. It didn't matter who excelled—the strong or the smart. What mattered was the fact that they were still alive. And if his group wanted to *stay* alive he realized that he and Larry would have to put aside their differences, like before, and work together in order to get through what lay ahead.

But first they needed the rain to stop.

They couldn't go anywhere in that rain.

Simon slumped down in the back seat, listening to the sound of the caustic liquid biting the windshield. He closed his eyes, let out a long, shuddering breath, and recited the first line of a nursery rhyme he hadn't heard in ages: "Rain, rain, go away.

"Please…"

And The River Rolled

Connor Rice

I haven't been the same since they passed away. My dear wife and son... It had been quick you see... car accidents often are... the screech of tires... the overpoweringly bright headlights and finally the sickly dull thump of grinding metal.

Emergency sirens, failed resuscitations, and my screams of loss– these were the kind of things that people heard that night.

You wouldn't know my real name but my fans know me as Chessler Maton, an odd name to be sure but pen names often are. I write books, or should I say, I *wrote* books. My family's passing shattered me and I haven't typed nor written anything in the year since they've been gone.

The days mixed together and I languished away in my cabin in the rural areas of east Texas. I occasionally had visitors but I don't remember them – I don't remember much of this time except that I didn't leave.

It wasn't until my friend Davis "Monster Truck" Trucker dropped by that I left – something about "moving on and getting back in the saddle"... the man had a way with words that was hard to deny. He was rough and honest.

So it was, that I found myself on the banks of the Buffalo River, staring into its slow flowing calm water. The canoe I had rented was already loaded down with my camping equipment and supplies; the outfitter had been generous, assuring me that this canoe was one of their better models.

Davis stood beside me, sweating in the mid afternoon sun. I had been researching for one of my books when I met him. He had been an *Ice Road Trucker*. He never did tell me why he had quit – just that he never wanted to be anywhere close to snow ever again.

He was overweight living up to his nickname as the "Monster Truck." His sweat pooled everywhere under his shirt. He swatted at a mosquito before asking in his distinct drawl, "You're sure you don't want me to come with you?" I shook my head slowly. "It's like you said Davis, I need this… but I need to do it alone."

Maybe he got it–maybe he didn't – either way he accepted it. "Alright Chessler, just be careful. I'll be waiting for you when you take out." Davis was a man of few goodbyes and with those simple words he heaved himself into his truck and sped off, a trail of dust arising like ghosts in his wake.

I didn't immediately leave. Instead I sat on the edge of my canoe and took in my surroundings. The river was located in a canyon that tapered off into lazy mountain ranges on steady slopes of tree and brush, sometimes shooting straight upwards into tall limestone cliffs.

I was miles from anyone but I didn't feel fear – after all

I had been separated from the world for a long time. I took out my cellphone and glanced at the lack of signal on it before powering it down and dropping it into a waterproof bag along with my wallet.

I sighed and glanced up and down the rock strewn beach. The river rounded a bend after about three hundred yards and disappeared. No one else was on the beach, no one to force me to leave and take the journey laid out for me, no one to see me walk out and drown myself in the slow moving rolling ripples of the river. I shoved those thoughts into the back of my mind.

I walked forward and began pushing the canoe out into the water, stopping just long enough to heave myself into it. The water splashed and the canoe rocked a little bit and I grunted trying to balance myself, but within a few seconds I had found my equilibrium.

I looked over my supplies – ice chest, snack bag, tent and cooking equipment... everything was there. I reached down and grabbed my paddle, heaving it across my lap.

I sighed and closed my eyes. A vision of my wife and son sitting in the canoe entered my mind. I felt two tears slide out from between my eyes and run slowly down my cheeks. I was painfully aware of all the sounds around me – the lapping water, the tweets of birds, and another –a disturbing sound.

My eyes snapped open and I listened intently before looking up river. A few cliffs jutted out from my side of the river imposing and wondrous. The sound came from the top, a man stood there waving a hand – I couldn't put my finger on it but he looked... ragged.

He was shouting something that I couldn't make out; I

strained to hear him when he put down his hand. He stopped shouting– instead he sat and stared. I felt uncomfortable… something was off about him. It came as shock when he turned and walked away slowly until he was out of sight.

I looked at the spot for a minute or two then slowly put it out of my mind before dipping my paddle into the river and shoving off from the bank in a crunch of gravel. The river current was strong here and it swiftly carried me away. The water was a light green– clear enough to see the massive amounts of rocks lining the riverbed.

Trees on the lazy mountains lined the side of the river – their roots spiraling down into the water and birds flew in and out and around me singing their songs. I went over white water and around boulders and under cliffs with ivy dangling like a net across the stone face, droplets falling like tears into the body of the river.

Sometimes the river turned dark green – its deepness all encompassing. The sun beat down on my skin and when the sweat pooled, I stopped to take a dip in the cool water. Time flew past me and before I knew it, the sun hung low in the sky.

***

I made camp on a lonely beach next to the river; the current was slow so to me, the river looked like it wasn't moving at all, not even the waves lapped against the shore. I paddled my canoe over to the beach, the gravel squelching as I pulled up. I swiftly jumped out of the canoe and hauled it up onto the land.

I made sure that the boat was high enough out of the water to not be in any danger of the tides carrying it off. I took my camping equipment out and began to assemble my tent.

I laid out the tent pegs on the edge of the canoe before reaching in and unloading the box that contained my tent. I found a spot that was flat enough and devoid of the rocks that made up the shoreline. I set to work and it wasn't long before the tent was completely assembled.

It was a blue and orange model big enough to fit two people comfortably. It wasn't long before I had laid my deflated air mattress inside and had attached the automatic inflator to the intake.

A steady whir filled the air as the inflator went to its task; I stood up with a sigh and looked at my home for the night. The forest loomed dark and imposing about thirty yards from my tent and in the opposite direction the water stood still and green. The sky and the swiftly fading sun reflected in its ripple-less sheen. Beyond that, a cliff wall loomed ominously upwards – another forest perched atop it.

I began stacking stones to make a fire pit and then went about collecting kindling. I walked closer to the trees finding plenty of small dead twigs lining the ground. It took several trips but I eventually had enough to start a small blaze.

The fire was small – barely born – but in no time, it was able to stand on its feet and began consuming the dead wood I fed to it. My air mattress was ready and my camp was set so I took it as time to begin settling in for the night. I changed into a long sweatshirt and long pajama pants. While it may have been the beginning of summer, it would no doubt become cold as the breeze blew in from over the water.

I unfolded a chair and sat my ice chest down beside me, unpacking the steak inside before laying it over the grate I had set across the fire. The meat immediately began to sizzle. I leaned back in my chair and just stared as the sun went down behind the mountains, the sky turning pink and then blue as the darkness closed in around me. I couldn't see anything beyond the light that my campfire provided and at that point I felt very much alone.

The mouth-watering smell of the meat wrapped around me and soon I forgot my misgivings and simply sat back and waited for my dinner to be ready. I didn't have to wait long before I was digging into the meat – savoring every last scrap that dropped down my throat, I moved onto the potatoes slowly and with much relish.

The meal was delicious and when I was through, I sat back and watched the firelight bounce off the cliffs in front me – the shadows dancing and entwining with each other in tune with the crackling of the flames.

I began making mental notes of things that I really liked about this place intending on setting my next book on the river – that is when I heard the first thump. It was a slow thing... just a dull thump coming from the direction of the river and echoing off the cliff face.

My eyes snapped open attempting to discern the cause of the sound. Another thump sounded and then another... every few seconds – like a heartbeat. I stood out of my chair and made my way towards the river. The thumps didn't get louder nor dwindle into silence – they simply continued beating low and dull.

The fire crackled behind me as I stood on the edge of the river squinting into the darkness. The water remained still, dark and eerily calm. I looked at the cliff wall – the light reflecting off it – then back down at the water. Whatever the thumps were, it was coming from under the water.

The muse inside of me remarked to me that this was it… the *heart* of the river and I was privileged to hear it. I shrugged off the thought and told myself that there must be an underwater current dragging boulders across the river bottom. The notion comforted me but as I looked back at the black water I felt unnerved. Deep inside me, the thought echoed to step into the water and let it roll over me.

I backed up slowly from the river – the thumps echoing after me. The fire was beginning to die down as I began packing up all of my cooking utensils and dirty dishes. The darkness began to close in further like a smothering blanket as I scrambled into my tent, zipping the fabric up as fast as I could as the last embers of flame flickered away.

I lay on the air mattress shaking in a state of near panic. After a few minutes my heart slowed down its staccato-like beat and began to take on a more regular rhythm. I slowly shut my eyes and tried to let sleep come and take me. I could still hear the thumps pounding incessantly and uninterrupted from the river… I could have sworn they had gotten faster.

***

I woke up early in the morning – right before the first light of day had begun to peak its way over the mountains. The first thing I was aware of was the lack of thumps. I slowly unzipped my tent and looked around the landscape. My fire pit, full of ash, was still where I had left it and nothing was amiss.

The early morning was grey and foggy and a low mist was hanging over the water – hazy clouds sweeping through the canyon. Birds chirped their morning song and somewhere, a crow caw echoed. I thought back to the night before and shrugged, chuckling to myself. That's the bad thing about

159

writers – we tend to have overactive imaginations.

I went to work making my breakfast – pouring out the pancake batter into my skillet. Pancakes were my addiction. My wife had made them for years to satiate my appetite. The food slid down my throat with surprising ease. I had never been the best cook and was surprised at my own skill. Hot black coffee chased the food – bitter and burned, but enough to wake me up. My eyes, previously heavy from a lack of sleep, snapped open as the liquid warmth ran rampant through my veins, comforting me and easing my muscles. By the time I was finished with breakfast the sun was just beginning to peak over the cliffs.

I got dressed – first putting on a red sleeveless shirt and blue and white swim trunks with a wide brimmed hat covering my head. I began to disassemble my camp–packing everything away–deflating my air mattress and finally disassembling the tent. Everything took a good forty-five minutes and when I was done, the canyon was alight with sunlight the water sparkling green.

I packed everything in the canoe and began shoving it down to the waterline. I hoisted myself into the boat and began the next leg of my journey. I turned around one last time to take in my campsite. Tiny vestiges of smoke were still drifting up from my dead campfire before it was lost to sight as I rounded the river bend.

I swiftly found myself bouncing from rapid to rapid – the swift moving water rushing me along like a freight train bouncing and bounding. I narrowly missed underwater boulders and fallen trees but through it all I laughed having fun in spite of myself.

I got out and swam at more than one point, letting the

cool water rush over me. I traveled miles. At one point a tiny waterfall trickled and splashed down an overhanging rock. Outcropping, I steered my canoe under it and closed my eyes. It was the coldest water I had ever felt – like I had been baptized and made new.

It wasn't until the middle of the day that I saw someone. I came to a set of rapids only to discover a beach with a campsite set up. It was obviously a family – two teenagers, an older child I was guessing with a wife, and a mom and dad. They were swimming and playing in the water dunking and splashing and obviously having a good time.

I tried to paddle by without saying a word but they waved me over, shouting for my attention.

"Good morning friend. Have you had good water today?" the man asked me an eager smile.

I slapped on the best fake smile I could muster and nodded in reply. "It's been tough in places though that might just be my lack of skill."

The man stood waist deep in the water, the current was strong and I fought to maintain my position in front of him, he chuckled at my remark before extending his hand. "Ryan Cummings."

I shook it back, rocking my canoe slightly. "Chessler Maton."

The man's eyes went wide. "The author?"

I nodded, a bemused smirk on my face. He immediately went into super fan mode, describing my books in detail, asking my take on parts– generally all the things that fans do.

I eventually cut in saying, "Ryan as much as I appreciate this praise of my work, it is getting difficult to sit here when the river is trying to hustle me on my way."

"I'm sorry Mr. Maton... um would you care to pull over and maybe join us for a while...? If we aren't keeping you from something that is."

I looked down the river then I looked at my hopeful fan in front of me. "Sure why not?"

I had been dead on with the fact that it was his family. I had even been right about their genders and marriages – they were all big fans of my work and I quickly warmed to them in return. They asked me questions about my books but most of the time they just let me be and treated me like I was one of them.

Ryan and his wife Cora knew about my loss. I was grateful that they only mentioned it once and apologized for bringing up something hurtful. It was a good afternoon and I found myself filling with tears as I waved goodbye and paddlcd away to find my own campsite.

The Cummings had asked me to stay though I had declined. I preferred my solitude and this trip was supposed to be about healing – not bringing my misery down on such a happy family.

I pulled up to a beach as the darkness closed in. The sky was already taking on the deep blue of early night and I hastily tried to get a fire going in the dark. Eventually, I had my entire campsite assembled and was relaxing in comfort – my air mattress blowing up in the dark–the steady whir a kind noise to my ears. I had set up on a long beach on the left side of the river – a long cliff wall ran the length of the beach. To the left of my camp, a set of white water rapids separated my beach from a rocky island full of short, sparse trees.

I had eschewed cooking in favor of a turkey and mushroom sandwich followed by a package of chips while relaxing in my chair and watching as the stars and moon carved places for themselves in the heavens. I breathed out a sigh when I heard the first thump. My head immediately snapped towards the river as the rhythmic thumping started again. I snarled and ran towards the waterline, flashlight in hand… the thumping continued steady and unyielding. I didn't know what to think! Twice in two nights couldn't be a coincidence but I couldn't find the source of the damned noise.

Even as I watched, the thumps began to slowly recede – moving away from me. I followed. I kept pace with it. My footsteps made a crunching sound crunching over the rocks. Together with the thumps, it sounded oddly like laughter.

It finally stopped moving at the rapids. The white water mixed in with the sound of thumping creating a noise like a train thundering by. I shone the flashlight over the water– the light bouncing back and forth – but I still couldn't find the source of the thumping.

The noise continued and I felt anger like it was mocking me *and* my efforts to find it. I would show it. I turned and walked back towards my campsite. I rubbed my eyes trying to think – the flashlight beam bounced off the ground as I walked. I shined it back towards the campsite and stopped dead in my tracks.

A man stood next to my tent… and he was smiling.

I took off at a dead run – the flashlight beam hitting the

ground only for a split second, but when I shined it back, the man was gone. I didn't stop running until I had made it to the camp. I looked everywhere but there was no one to be found. I sat there in silence – the only sound coming from the ever present thumping down the beach.

I got the sense I was being watched. I looked at the dark woods seeing nothing – no noise coming from the wooden sentinels. After I calmed down, I began to think of all the possibilities, hoping that my mind was just overreacting. I put my chair up against my tent and sat staring at the fire (though I stoked it), attempting to drown out the faint thumping I could still hear.

The fire roared to life as I fed it and eventually the crackling and popping of the flames drowned out the thumps. I sighed and sat back, watching the flickering light dance and bounce across the cliff face.

The light twisted and turned and I thought I could make out the shadow of my tent on the stone; I sat up and stared – other shadows joined in forming people. I looked all across the beach looking for the source of the shadows but there was no one to cast them.

Another shadow joined them; he had an axe in his hand. I watched as he killed each of them stabbing them, clubbing them with a large stick–all of it merely shadows from my fire. I sat entranced and horrified at what I was seeing and when it was finished, the shadow of the man stood alone on the cliff wall unmoving.

I scrambled back to my tent as quickly as I could. My hands were fumbling to unzip it. My wife was sitting on the air mattress.

I stared at her as she patted the fabric. "Come to bed dear."

I shook my head back and forth. "You aren't real I'm hallucinating."

"Come to bed dear," she said again.

I stumbled back from the tent and felt a tiny hand grab mine and a small voice whisper, "Daddy."

I closed my eyes muttering to myself, "Make it stop, make it stop, make it stop."

I felt my wife's hands on my chest.

"Yesterday you saw a man who wasn't there. He wasn't there again today... but we are never going away," she said.

I snapped. My voice erupted from my mouth, "STOP!" The hands on my chest and the one in my hand vanished. I opened my eyes and looked around. I was alone on the beach standing in the dark... the fire had been extinguished...

***

I lay in my tent for the rest of the night not moving – just listening. The thumps echoed through the night but I could swear I heard footsteps on the edge of the woods pacing back and forth – taunting me.

I don't know when sleep took me, but when I awoke I was still inside my tent. I immediately sat up and looked around. I had slept late as I could already see the sunlight blazing outside the fabric. I unzipped my tent and looked around – nothing was amiss, everything still in the same place I left it.

I stepped out of the tent and immediately had to close my eyes. The sun seemed closer, more menacing. I could barely see the edges of the sky over the bright yellow orb and even then they were yellow as well.

I immediately unpacked my sunscreen and went about applying it to my body – the white liquid blending in with my skin. Flies buzzed all around my campsite alighting on my half-finished meal from the previous night that lay where I had dropped it. I didn't even bother trying to pick it up as I packed up the camp. I tried to get away from the beach as soon as possible. I was soon pushing the canoe into the water – my muscles aching at my urgency – but I soon left the accursed place behind.

I wasn't sure what to think about my night. In my entire year I had never imagined nor hallucinated about my wife and child yet they had been there last night as real as anything else. They had felt solid until I wished them away.

I had wished them away… the thought hit me like a sledgehammer – what if they were back and I had thrown them away? What if they were trying to contact me? These questions ran through my mind as the river carried me slowly over the next mile of my journey. I would occasionally look up at the sky – the sun was overpowering but it still hung there lazy and rotten like an open sore. I could have sworn it hadn't moved since I woke up that morning.

There were no white water or rapids today. The water remained deep green and dark – my thoughts drifted back to the previous night… what if I was going crazy? I didn't feel crazy, but didn't all crazy people think that?

I realized at that point I didn't hear any birds – or any noise for that matter, except for the occasional splash as my paddle dipped into the water. It was unnerving traveling through this silent world. Trying to do something that would take my mind off of the world around me, I unpacked my fishing pole.

I smiled as the memory of the fishing trip with my son filled my mind. I took my first cast. The bait flew through the air landing with a heavy plop into the water. I reeled it in without any bites before trying again. I repeated the process time after time with no bites signaling a fish but I didn't care... the action soothed me. I sat like that all afternoon – drifting, casting; reeling... it came almost as a surprise when the line tugged back.

I jumped in my seat as I felt the line tighten and begin to move back and forth – the fish testing its will against my own. It dove, twisted, and came ever closer as I worked to reel it in foot by foot, the line slowly winding its way back inside the rod. I had it beside the boat but the fish hadn't breached the surface. It tugged back hard making me look over into the water. A hand clutched my line – its forearm running down into the water connecting to my reflection like it was reaching out of the water... only it wasn't my reflection – something else stared back at me, something undulating and wrong. The reflection reached up and tapped on the side of the canoe three times... thump, thump, thump.

I recoiled from the sight and sound, falling out of the canoe in the process. Sputtering water, I breached the surface looking around for anything unusual. Nothing moved nor swam in the cold water. I didn't take any chances as I reached up and grabbed my canoe, hauling it over to the nearest beach and crawling out.

I stood and scanned the water but there was no trace of

the strange reflection that had given me my tumble. I sat breathing hard looking up and down the beach – a small patch of color caught my eye, different, unnatural under the blaring sun.

I jogged down the beach toward it– the mass occasionally twitched or rolled unnaturally, causing me to hesitate as I drew near. What I saw made me want to vomit – it was a corpse bloated and rotted by what looked like a massive amount of time immersed in water. Crawfish crawled in and out of the corpse and I could see more of them moving under the skin and through the exposed ribcage.

The corpse was wearing a torn red shirt and shredded blue swim trunks… the exact same thing I was wearing. "What's going on?" I screamed at the sky, the sun fat and bloated and staring down at me, but no one answered.

I felt weak and tired. I dropped to my knees and then sat on the rocks, staring at the corpse wondering who it was and dreading the answer. The sun still beat down heavily as I closed my eyes but when I opened them, night had descended and the darkness hung all around me.

I scrambled to my feet looking at the sky – no moon, no stars. The sun had been there one moment and then it hadn't. The corpse was gone too. My half asleep mind made me think it had walked away while my rational mind said it had slipped back into the water… of course what was rational about this situation?

I hastily began making a fire desperate for light – any kind of light to stem the darkness around me. The fire barely pushed back – the light hardly giving me enough to work with as I set up my tent. Eventually I gave up. What was the point? Nothing was right here – something I couldn't explain had dominance over my life.

I sat staring at the fire thinking and wondering what to do. When I eventually looked up, the thumps had started once again. I covered my ears and began muttering over and over again "Go away, go away, go away..." Of course they never went away.

I stood and began pacing around the fire trying to think – to reason through the situation. It didn't take long to notice something different. Far away down the beach another fire flickered, warm and inviting just out of sight around the bend of the beach.

I began running down the beach, desperate for any form of contact. I quickly worked up a sweat as I made my way down the sandy water's edge – the gravel and rocks crunched beneath my feet, the dark trees flashed by, the evening wind whipped past me cooling me down, and the thumps followed me beating in time to my footfalls.

I ran for twenty minutes before I realized the truth – the fire around the bend wasn't getting any closer. It looked the same distance away as it did before. I felt like I had run at least two miles. I was out of breath – my sweat coating my clothes and skin. I knew what I would see when I turned around but it shocked me nonetheless. My camp was only about thirty yards behind me – fire still blazing the way I had left it twenty minutes ago. Wearily I walked back over and fell down on the rocks staring up into the immense blackness of the sky, just feeling tired. Very tired.

***

I didn't want to move. I didn't want to think. I just wanted everything to stop, as I lay uncomfortable on the stones – the fire seeming to provide light but no warmth. My sweat was cold – the adrenaline having worn off in the time I had spent lying down.

I sat and thought about the next day and what I had to look forward to – another day of misery canoeing down a river that had turned from a wondrous catharsis to another nightmare AND another night of uncertainty and eerie events.

"Screw this," I muttered to myself as I stood up. I wasn't going to go through another day of this mind screw. I went to my canoe – the fire flickering behind me and opened up one of the boxes, digging through everything inside, not caring what I tossed out or what I lost – until – I found what I was looking for.

The flashlight was a comfort in my hands – its light piercing the darkness. The map was my lifeline out of here. I walked past the fire and the half constructed tent until I stood before the shadow infested forest. The light barely penetrated but I was determined to get out of this nightmare.

With the deepest breath I could muster, I plunged into the tree line. The branches whipped around me, the sticks and leaves cracking and crunching under my feet. I proceeded uphill occasionally stopping to check the map route. A town was over the canyons walls only a couple of miles away – all things considered.

I stopped to rest often leaning up against trees – scouting the darkness for God knows what, but nothing revealed itself to me. A few hours later I was at the top of the mountain. I looked back down and could see my fire still burning far below. I laughed and began hiking down the other side – the river becoming lost to sight.

The hike down wasn't nearly as arduous as the hike up had been and I soon found myself just lazily trying to avoid the large boulders – the trees having widened out, I laughed and whistled to myself as I walked feeling good, feeling relieved, seeing it as nothing more than a short lived nightmare.

The trees became thick again but I knew that a road would be on the other side – I felt it. I stopped when I emerged from the forest and found my campsite staring back at me. The fire was crackling just as high as when I had left it – my half built tent still in shambles on the ground.

My knees felt weak but I didn't sit. Instead I began giggling and laughing. I was laughing so hard that my stomach hurt but I didn't notice as a feeling of helplessness and hopelessness washed over me like the river water. I kept laughing as I walked down to my canoe and pulled out the small hatchet. I ran forward and began hacking at the dark water screaming inarticulate rage at what I blamed for my predicament.

Despite the water, I was sweating – the exertion getting to me. The thumps were still sounding out but now they beat fast like a drum. At first everything was silent and smooth across the dark water, but then it began churning – a splashing and foaming only about thirty yards away – then something stood up out of the water and began making its way towards me.

I turned and ran past the fire and the tent that was plunging back into the woods, with my flashlight and hatchet not wanting to look or even acknowledge whatever it was that was following me. Faces flashed around me–faces that I knew. My son, my wife, my friends, the Cummings, all of their faces flashing by their eyes rippling like pools of water each of them knocking on the trees as I flew by… thump, thump, thump.

I began screaming – a scream of rage, loss, and fear. The tree limbs reached for me, whipping past me with deadly speed, cutting my skin – the blood released flowing across my body and dropping to the ground a red trail of sorrow. I saw light through the trees – the figures all around me turned at it with looks of disdain filling their corrupt features. Slowly, they faded into the trees, leaving me alone.

I was cautious – not trusting my senses. I crept slowly forward – I heard laughter, crunching rocks, and the thumps. Something inside me knew that it was another trap just designed to lure me in and make me question my sanity once again but I wanted so desperately to see something else something human.

I plunged out of the woods, hatchet in hand. A campsite laid before me, the river beyond that. The five individuals stopped what they were doing and turned to look – my wife, my son, Davis Trucker, my agent, and my editor all sat around a fire looking at me – their skin bloated and swollen – their eyes dark pools of water.

They looked shocked then they began laughing. I smiled back and began laughing too –eyeing a solid length of dead oak by the fire. I walked over to it still smiling and picked it up acting as if I were about to toss it into the fire.

Instead I turned and hit the monstrosity that looked like my wife across the face with it. I buried my hatchet into the one that looked like my editor. I tore and carved and beat at the aberration – my anger and tenuous grasp on reality were offended that these things would take the form of the people I loved. The actions were alien to me but familiar at the same time.

They made noises that could have been pleading but I didn't care – I kept hammering away at them until they ceased moving. Water leaked out of their bodies coating the rocks and running down towards the river. I sat by the fire attempting to warm myself and rubbing my hands to create friction. I laughed to myself, reveling in my triumph – a laugh that was stopped when a wet splashing noise caught my ear.

I looked down to the river – the water leaking from the bodies swirled and splashed on the rocks writhing, undulating, and slowly taking shape. I watched in horror as another body formed, wearing a red shirt and blue swim trunks. When it was over, I saw my own face staring back at me only with deep rippling pools of water for eyes.

It walked toward me and slowly crouched on the other side of the fire from me. It didn't talk—it only stared at me. I stared back unnerved. The thing raised its hand and pointed towards the cliff wall on the other side of the river. The shadows moved there and in horror I realized why I had felt so comfortable and familiar killing the monsters. The shadows were the same pageant of silent horror I had stared at two nights ago on another canyon wall.

I looked down at my hands and dropped the hatchet and club in shock; the thing across from me smiled a smile that was larger than anything a human could possibly make, psychotic and evil. It pointed at the bodies and it was like a veil had been ripped from eyes – they didn't look like my loved ones anymore… I looked at the dead bodies of the Cummings – each one dead and gone – the blood running red on the stones.

"No," I whispered to myself. The thing across from me

pointed right at me and whispered a word that I dreaded to hear: "Guilty."

"NOOO!" I screamed and threw the hatchet. It struck the thing in the chest causing it to explode in a shower of water that rained down upon me.

"No, no, no," I repeated the word over and over again as I stood up and staggered away into the darkness.

***

The night wheeled overhead and I stumbled around with no light to guide me, having lost all rationality and intent. Only one sound accompanied me… thump, thump, thump.

When I finally came back to myself, I found that I was standing in front of my campsite and that blackest night had changed to an overpoweringly hot and bright day. I looked up at the sky – the sun was as red as blood, bathing the world in a red sheen, bloated and swollen like a tick.

I ran on sheer panic, packing up my supplies and tossing them haphazardly into the canoe. I eased into the water and began rowing down the river. The water had changed from the deep dark green to an oily black, impenetrable and unknowing; the thumps followed me in the day –now a never-ending staccato in my ears.

The black water clung to my paddle, sticking like oil before running back down into the main body of water. I kept going somewhere – anywhere that I could find people. Fish floated dead on the water all around me – their lifeless eyes staring at me with accusation and knowing; each one had the word *Guilty* carved into it.

I paddled through them, trying not to touch them and failing to do so. The fish floated all around me and then I saw the first corpse; it was floating face down, bobbing like an upended cork. I turned it over with my paddle and saw the face of Ryan Cummings looking back at me – his throat leaking fresh blood.

The water began moving faster and the number of corpses increased each one of them with the face of someone I knew. They floated so thick on the water that I couldn't see the river underneath them. The sounds of them sliding across the boat were unnerving, like sandpaper running across a tabletop.

I shut my eyes, feeling the tears running down my face. I let the water carry me for hours, not opening my eyes afraid of what I would see. A bubbling, roaring sound reached my ears and I opened them up to see a large waterfall straight ahead of me – corpses tumbling and falling over it.

I frantically tried to paddle backwards but it wasn't any use. I let out one long scream as I tumbled over the edge. I fell for a few seconds before hitting the water. I sank down– the black water warm around me. More corpses floated under the water and no matter where I moved, their hands rubbed across me, their faces staring. A stream of bubbles escaped my mouth as I screamed under the water and clawed frantically for the surface.

I breached the surface gasping for air, looking frantically around. Corpses littered the water all around me but my canoe only floated a few yards away. I swam for it, pushing the dead out of the way and hauled myself into the boat, finally resting in the floor of the boat shivering and whimpering.

The boat didn't move the water was too thick with corpses to allow it. Instead, the boat sat marooned in a sea of the dead. The thumps kept pounding and I screamed and ranted for them to go away but whatever powers that ruled this world felt no need to answer me.

I rose from my fetal heap and looked at a paddle that lay floating a few yards away. I reached for it and began trying to make my way out of this hell. The corpses were stubborn. I had to move each one with the paddle, trying hard not to notice – the chill bumps racing down my body.

I looked around trying to ascertain where I was. Instead I asked myself the only sane question I could think of– "What the hell?" My entire trip so far had been something out of a nightmare and now it looked like it had been crossed with something from a surrealism painting.

The limestone cliffs to my right jutted straight out of the water, tall and imposing. Corpses hung off rocks and were impaled on the sparse trees that had found a place to call home. At the base of the cliffs were two large caves halfway out of the water – corpses filling the entrances like pus from a wound.

To my left was beach bordered by more cliffs but on that beach laid cars of all models and an eighteen-wheeler overturned on its side. The red sunlight fell down all around me, bouncing off the abandoned pieces of machinery and illuminating the water of the lagoon I sat in blood red.

I paddled over to the shore and slowly got out. Nothing moved over the beach – nothing came to meet me and for the first time since I had arrived on this river, the thumps no longer came from the river. They came from somewhere amongst the strewn cars, inviting me. I followed the sound hesitantly, dreadfully, unsure of what I was expecting to find. I walked past cars on all sides of me – sticking out of the sand and rocks like massive tombstones. With the red sunlight pouring down I felt like I was in a blood drenched graveyard.

The thumps grew louder and louder until I could pinpoint where they were coming from– it was a small Dodge Stratus– something that wasn't out of the ordinary to most people but I recognized this car. It had been my car.

Everything about it was the same, down to the small dents acquired from people opening doors too quickly and chipping the paint. Flashes of my family smiling, happy, alive flooded my thoughts and I started breathing hard I tried to bring myself under control, forcing myself to breathe slowly and surely. My chest felt like a massive animal was sitting atop it, crushing my ribs and sucking all the air out of my lungs, an inescapable weight that I was powerless to stop.

The back of the car thumped and banged drawing my attention away from my struggles. I stepped forward and stared down as the trunk of the car banged and quivered begging to be opened and revealed. My hands trembled as I reached down and pressed the trunk release – it popped open with a loud bang.

My wife and son were in the back of the trunk smiling – their eyes dark black pools of water. Rope bound their hands together – my wife said, "We've been waiting for you dear."

I backed up shaking my head; my son stood up and walked towards me, bound hands reaching.

"What's wrong Dad? This isn't what you wanted remember?"

I shook my head, "No, no this shit isn't real."

My wife was suddenly behind me – her bound hands clutching my arm, her tongue extending to lick the lobe of my ear sending a wave of chill bumps and nausea down my body.

"But you did sweet pea... ever since our son was born, you complained that you weren't getting enough time to write, that we were taking up too much effort, that we were holding you back."

I tried to jump away from her but my son's body was suddenly behind me, his hands holding my arm tight.

"Then the night came when you decided you just couldn't live with us anymore Dad," he said.

I strained against their hold and when they let go, I fell sprawling into the gravel and sand. I coughed as the sand scratched its way down my throat turning over to find my wife lying down beside me – her arms reaching across caressing my chest.

"So you drugged us, Chessler... we fell blissfully into our last sleep and you tied us up and put us in the trunk... we weren't supposed to wake up but we did."

My son crouched over me. "We pounded on the trunk lid, but you laughed as the car rolled into the lake – you heard us scream but it was the thumps that stayed with you like the tell-tale heart."

I lay there frozen. It wasn't true – couldn't be true – I'd never murder my wife and son... would I? None of this made sense. The voice at the back of my mind whispered... *what were you thinking? You've gone crazy; you've lost it, completely wacko.*

I would know if I was crazy wouldn't I? I mean crazy people often knew when they stepped over that edge into insanity didn't they? I didn't feel insane– I felt afraid.

"The only car crash was the big rig that killed you Dad… the big rig that struck you after you murdered us."

The red sun blazed and beat like a giant heart and then began melting, oozing out of the sky like bloody snot – large plops of red rain dropping into the black river water. The corpses floating in it began moving and quivering twitching as the red droplets entered their skin. Then they began screaming.

My wife's whisper was louder than the awful din.

"You know you're guilty, Chessler, you know you deserve this…" She gestured around as I whispered, "Where am I?"

Her hand moved down grasping my man hood in a perverse display, "This is hell, Chessler, welcome home."

Something in my mind snapped and I screamed a scream of inarticulate rage, grief, and denial. I kicked the thing that looked like my son away and rolled over on top of my wife. She only smiled as my hands wrapped around her throat. The thumps began pounding fast like jungle tribe music.

"I murdered you once, I'll do it again. You wanted me baby, well here I am!" I put all my weight into my arms and fingers, my wife quivered under me her tongue lolling out of her mouth.

She didn't fight back she only stroked my arms and chest, between gasps I heard her whisper, "Faster baby, faster."

I held my breath as I felt her neck break like a small stick in my hands. The thumps began slowing dying. I kept holding it as her quivering ceased… my vision fading as blood vessels burst…

***

I came to in my canoe, holding a broken wooden paddle in my hands. I wasn't sure what to think at first. The river ran below me – a cool blue so clear I could see the fish at the bottom. The sun had just cleared one of the mountains ahead of me, its golden rays lighting the mist hovering above the water. It seemed like I was floating through golden fog.

The sun wasn't beating nor bleeding. The sky wasn't red. Cars didn't line the sides of the beach like tombstones – only trees and cool rushing water. Everything looked normal and beautiful.

There were no thumps, no corpses, nothing but wonderful nature. I laughed and splashed myself with the broken paddle and began screaming, "It was all in my head."

The joy in my voice real enough to touch, I found my fishing pole and began to cast rhythmically. Every few casts I pulled in a fish. I pulled out my stringer and hooked the fishes through the gills pulling them behind the boat.

I didn't understand how all my supplies were still in my boat; something had obviously happened – the tent was still ripped and my clothes were still dirty and torn but I wasn't injured, just tired.

I asked myself if it all could have been a dream – a dream so vivid I had slept walked and packed up my canoe.

No answer seemed to ring true in my mind and eventually I gave up thinking about it – decided that I just didn't care. It was over and that was all I cared about.

Gradually the blue sky grew thick grey clouds and low rumbles of thunder split the air. Then the sky cracked open and large, warm droplets fell down – I opened my mouth taking them in, grateful for fresh real rain. Life seemed brighter–more real than I had ever seen it before. The trees were greener, the water bluer, and the stones more solid… I was going to live so much after this trip – maybe write a new book. Everything I had gone through would definitely make a hell of a story.

I paddled for hours until I came to a wide stretch of river where the water could only have been a few feet deep. The sunlight illuminated the water making it as clear as staring into thin air, like I was floating on a sea of liquid glass.

I reached down with my paddle touching the river bottom and stirring up both dust and minnows. I laughed, having a good time and when I looked up. I found that my journey had reached its end.

The river abruptly ended ahead– something I didn't remember from the map, but it looked like the water had dropped low enough to expose dry ground. Canoes were pulled up all along the bank of the river. I didn't see anyone around to take the canoes, nor did I see Davis Trucker waiting for me.

A large sloping cliff separated this tiny beach from what I assumed was the rest of the river. It had a natural staircase that I decided I was supposed to climb and meet with the boat porter and my friend. I made sure my canoe wasn't going to float away before walking up the rock steps. Every step felt like an ascension from hell to heaven and I had found redemption. I was stepping out of the watery pit to the rocky heavens.

I came over the cliff side and found myself surrounded by trees and boulders and a jutting cliff to my right which led all the way down into the water. Lying before me was a beach and a rolling river. A truck sat out of place along with Davis Trucker waiting on me. He was talking to another man with a canoe that I assumed had to be one of the canoe rental company employees. I sat smiling – just taking it in for a moment. It was odd being at the end of my journey after everything that had happened. There was something familiar about it, despite it being new.

I watched Davis talk to the man. It looked like the conversation was reaching its end. Davis Trucker shook the man's hand but then something else happened... Davis left. He walked heaving and quivering to the truck and hoisted himself into it.

"WAIT!" I shouted at the top of my lungs jogging forward, but the truck sped off leaving a long cloud of dust in its wake.

I rocked on my feet slightly wondering why my friend had left. Had he not seen me? Did he not know to wait?

I looked at the other man on the beach thinking he looked familiar. He stood on the beach staring at God knows what for the longest time and I sat watching him unsure of what to do.

It wasn't until he began pushing the canoe on the beach out into the water that I became concerned. I shouted at the man at the top of my lungs but he didn't turn around. He sat balancing inside his canoe. I shouted again waving my arms in the air and this time he turned around… it was only then that I realized what he was wearing… a red shirt and blue swim trunks.

I stared at myself and he stared back at me – the end at the beginning. I stopped waving and instead I just stared back unnerved. Something cracked inside me. I turned away from myself and walked away, sitting on a rock out of sight of the river. I sat there staring at nothing in particular, thinking of nothing in particular, when a hand touched my shoulder. I looked up and my wife stood beside me – her neck still caved in from my hands – her features bloated and distorted – her eyes rippling pools of dark water.

"You couldn't leave us that easily, Chessler."

I nodded. "I know."

She smiled back knowingly. "You know what you have to do to be with us."

I nodded again. "I do."

She smiled back gracefully and beautifully. I looked over her again and she transformed from death to life, beautiful and whole. "Come home Chester."

I stood up and walked to the cliff edge and stared down into the water, lapping and inviting.

My son grabbed my hand. "Come be with us Daddy."

I stared once again down at the water dark and inviting and then I jumped. The dark water opened wide and yearning and I hit it like a stone, sinking down into its dark depths. I sank – the light fading above me…

And the river rolled…

The *Rose-Marie*

Jon Olson

Waves calmly rolled up along the beach and pulled back as if they were caressing the shore of Angel Island. Night had fallen and just a few meters away from the water's edge was a large campfire with a father and son sitting around it. The flames fluttered, casting dancing shadows across Jacob Fleming's face as he continued telling a ghost story to six year old Dawson.

"…And the fisherman could not believe his eyes," Jacob said in a low voice. "Floating in front of him was the dreaded *Rose-Marie*. At first he thought he was dreaming so he closed his eyes, wishing the image away, and then pinched himself but when he opened them again it was still there. The legendary fishing trawler that the fisherman had grown up hearing about was real."

Dawson was leaning forward in his Spiderman folding chair with his elbows on his knees and chin resting firmly in his hands, completely entranced by the story.

"According to the stories, the *Rose-Marie* had disappeared with her entire crew on board and not one of them was ever heard from again. For years, reports of *Rose-*

Marie sightings had spread like wildfire. The strange thing was no one had been able to locate it with the proper equipment to tow it back to shore. It was as if the vessel only appeared when it wanted to." Jacob paused for effect and tossed a small log onto the fire.

Dawson squirmed a little in his chair anxious for his father to continue, "And then what happened, Daddy?" he asked.

"The fisherman tried to radio for assistance but his radio would not work. He couldn't reach anyone and was alone. It was if the *Rose-Marie* herself was preventing him from making contact."

"Why?"

"She wanted him to be a member of her crew, needing fresh souls to operate it."

"So why didn't he just leave?"

"He tried, son. Oh how he tried but the engine just wouldn't start. He started to hear noises coming from the *Rose-Marie*. It started off as a faint moaning but as the volume increased he could hear cries of pain from deep within the ship's hull."

"Who was in the *Rose-Marie*, Daddy?" Dawson asked.

"Nobody was. You see son, the *Rose-Marie* was able to mimic the sounds of its victims. It would make the noises like someone was in pain or needed help to lure the next victim on board. The fisherman put his hands up to his ears to try to block out the wails but it was too much. He wanted it to stop but it wouldn't! And then…"

"RAAAHHHHH!"

Emily Fleming jumped out of the darkness screaming as she grabbed Dawson by the shoulders. Dawson let out a wail of fear, desperately trying to get out of her grasp until he looked and saw who it was. Seeing that it was his mother, he started to laugh while gasping to catch his breath. Emily hugged her son and kissed him on the cheek before taking her seat in the chair beside her husband.

Jacob threw another log onto the fire and the flames consumed it greedily. He leaned back in his chair and felt his wife's hands wrap around his left arm. She rested her head on his shoulder and he kissed the top of it while enjoying the smell of her hair. Through the flames he could see that Dawson was making a mess of what was once a marshmallow.

"Daddy?" Dawson asked. He put what was left of the marshmallow in his mouth, "Will you help me build a boat tomorrow?"

"Sure, but what for?"

"So I can look for the *Rose-Marie*." Dawson grinned at his father.

"You got it big guy."

The family of three was spending their first complete summer at their newly constructed cottage on Angel Island, just off the coast of British Columbia. The island itself was less than three kilometers long and two kilometers at its widest. Being incredibly successful in his career as an engineer and having friends in the right places, Jacob managed to lease the island from the province. Their cottage was decent sized with two bedrooms, kitchen, and living room with a wraparound porch. A large gas powered generator provided electricity for their refuge and aside from the dock and the half built shed in the back yard their cottage was the only other man-made structure on the island.

To get to Angel Island they had to charter a boat to bring them out as well as pick them up when they needed to replenish their supplies. They worked out a deal with Charlie Tippet, who owned the boat, to remain on call in case they had any emergencies that needed immediate action. Charlie could make it to the island in less than twenty minutes whereas the Coast Guard was almost an hour away by helicopter. They had a radio as well as Jacob's satellite phone but other than that they were cut off.

Jacob turned his head slightly and looked out at the Pacific Ocean, which was illuminated by a full moon. The ocean was relatively calm with a slight breeze. Aside from a couple of navigational buoys blinking along the horizon, there was nothing else in sight. Without even realizing it Jacob allowed his mind to be consumed by the vastness of the ocean.

His wife's voice returned his attention to the beach.

"Dawson, I think you've had enough marshmallows," she chuckled. "You look like you've gotten more on you than in you."

"Oh please, just one more, Mommy?" Dawson asked.

She looked at him then relented, "Alright, just one more. After that we get you inside, cleaned up and into bed."

"Thanks Mommy." Dawson's hands were already diving inside the bag of marshmallows at his feet.

Jacob smiled and turned out to the ocean again where something caught his eye. He stood up and gazed hard out at the horizon.

Quite far off shore he could make out what looked like to be a ship. There were no lights of any kind and he could not hear any sounds of an engine running. In fact there didn't seem to be any sort of activity associated with it. It was as if the ship was just drifting on its own without anyone steering it. Jacob scowled and immediately felt like there was something wrong with what he was looking at.

"What do you make of that?" Jacob asked.

Emily looked to where Jacob was facing and after a few seconds she saw it as well, "A boat?"

He gave her a playful dirty look, "Do you find it odd that it's just there with no lights on?"

"No not really. They could've just stopped for the night."

"I don't think they've stopped," Jacob said. "It looks like its drifting."

Emily looked at it a bit harder, "Not to me."

"Maybe I just find it odd that in the two weeks we've been here I don't recall seeing a single ship aside from the one that we arrived on."

"It's not a high traffic area," Emily said. "It's one of the main reasons we built this cottage out here." She stood up and kissed him on the cheek before turning her attention to Dawson. "Alright you destroyer of marshmallows, time to get cleaned up and ready for bed."

"Okay." Dawson said sounding a little disappointed. He stood up and carefully made his way around the campfire to his father. "Good night, Daddy."

Jacob knelt down, gave him a hug and kissed the only spot on his cheek that wasn't covered in marshmallow, "Good night, big guy. Sleep well."

"I won't be long." Emily said.

Jacob watched her walk away as she placed her hand between Dawson's shoulder blades leading him towards the cottage. She was wearing one of Jacob's football sweatshirts and a pair of white shorts over her red bikini. He was proud of her as she had managed to shed all of the weight she put on during Dawson's pregnancy and regained the body she had as a varsity athlete in university where they met. Once she and Dawson climbed the stairs on the porch and disappeared inside the cottage, he sat down.

He grabbed a stick and poked the fire with it, watching the flames as he did but soon found his mind wandering back to the boat.

To Jacob, it looked like it had gotten a little bit closer but it just could've been his eyes playing tricks on him as Emily had said that it didn't look like it was moving to her. He guessed it to be a fishing trawler like one of those crab boats he had seen on *Deadliest Catch*. Any sense of time vanished as he locked his eyes on it, not even hearing his wife walking up behind him. It wasn't until she spoke that he noticed she was there.

"He's out like a light," she said. She sat down on his lap and leaned her back into his chest. "Where did you get that story from?"

"Which?"

She elbowed him lightly in the stomach, "The *Rose-Marie*. I don't remember ever reading it in any of our ghost story books back home."

"Charlie Tippet told me about it," Jacob said. "Apparently the *Rose-Marie* is a real ghost ship."

"A real ghost ship?"

"That's what Charlie said," Jacob said. "When Japan was hit by that tsunami it washed a lot of debris out to sea with it including cars, pieces of buildings and boats. Just before we left home I read an article on how some of the debris was heading towards the coast of British Columbia. The Coast Guard actually spotted a large fishing vessel adrift with the debris and identified it as the *Rose-Marie*."

"That's kind of neat." Emily said.

"Odd thing was, the Japanese had no records of the boat ever being at any of its docks. Charlie said the *Rose-Marie* has only ever been spotted in ports or just off the shore of areas just before a natural disaster strikes."

"Now you're making that up," Emily said. "So the boat is like a precursor to natural disasters like what... hurricanes?"

Jacob shook his head, "Earthquakes and..."

"And what?"

"Tsunamis." Jacob said. "It had been spotted near Sri Lanka and Haiti as well as Japan right before they were hit."

Emily sat up, turned and looked at her husband, "Are you sure you're not letting your nightmare influence what you've been told?"

"No my dreams aren't influencing anything here," Jacob said raising his hands truthfully. "That's what Charlie said and while it's a good story I think he's exaggerating things a bit."

"I like your version better." Emily said leaning back into him.

"It was fun telling it."

They sat in silence for a few minutes; the only sounds that could be heard were the waves and the crackling of the fire. Emily tilted her head to look up at him and noticed he was looking back out towards the ocean. She looked out at it as well but found no interest in it so she stood up and turned around, straddling Jacob in the process. Her hands grasped the bottom of the sweatshirt and she pulled it over her head, revealing the red bikini top garnering Jacob's full attention.

"Do you find that boat more interesting than me?" she asked.

Feeling the rising bulge in his shorts pressing against her, Jacob slid his hands up her back and united her bikini top sliding it off in one fluid motion.

"Not even in the slightest." He said kissing her and they made love on the beach next to the dying fire.

***

Jacob didn't know when he acquired his fear of the water but it always carried over into his dreams. They always started out the same with his wife and son playing in the shallow waters of the Pacific Ocean while he looked on from the deck of a ship. They splashed each other, laughing, before Emily scooped Dawson up in her arms and hugged him.

Then it would happen.

The water would begin to recede from the beach, leaving Emily and Dawson suddenly standing on a sandbar where seconds ago it had been shallowly submerged. She would watch the water continue to pull back making a hideous sucking sound and then she'd shoot a concerned look up to Jacob. He then would motion for them to start coming back onto land but they just stood there.

The sucking sound would soon fade and a deathly silence hung in the air.

Then Jacob would hear it.

Faint at first, like a distant train rumbling down a set of steel tracks, but increasing at a rapid pace. Jacob would point to the ocean wall and start screaming.

A giant wall of water was rushing towards them with evident destructive intent.

Jacob would then yell as loud as he could for Emily and Dawson to run but they could not hear him. The rushing twelve meter high wave blocked out any sound and they just stood where they were like mannequins in a store window. Jacob would try to climb down off of the ship to run to save them but his legs were locked, unwilling to run towards his fear.

He was then forced to watch in horror as the tidal wave ran over his family like a massive bulldozer, erasing their existence.

The wave then continued to rush towards him and the boat he was on. Despite the nightmarish setting, one thing that always stuck out to him was he could never tell what boat he was on. He always woke up just as the wave struck him.

***

Jacob opened his eyes and for a moment did not recognize where he was. The ceiling of the cottage was an off-white and a fan attached to the light fixture slowly spun causing the pull chords to sway gently. He blinked a couple of times and without lifting it from his pillow, turned his head to his left and saw that Emily was looking at him.

"The same dream?" she asked.

"Just like always." Jacob said.

Emily reached over and held Jacob's hand in her own, "We didn't have to build our cottage here. We could've built one elsewhere."

"I wasn't going to let a silly fear of the water make decisions in my life," Jacob said. "We all love it out here and it's something that I'm just going to have to get over."

"Mommy! Daddy!" Dawson's voice sounded distant.

Jacob looked to his right at the clock beside the bed and saw that it was 6:37 am.

"He's up early," Jacob said.

They heard Dawson running up the porch steps and then the front screen door squeaked open. Dawson's footsteps thudded throughout the cottage, getting louder as they got closer to the bedroom. The door opened and he poked his head in the room out of breath.

"Daddy, you have to get up and see!" Dawson's eyes were wide with excitement.

"See what?" Jacob asked sitting up.

"The ghost ship!"

"The what?"

"The *Rose-Marie*, Daddy," Dawson started to run back outside. "It's here!"

"He's getting your talent for stories," Emily joked.

Jacob swung his feet onto the floor, reached down and grabbed a pair of shorts. He stood up and stumbled out of the bedroom into the living room where he stretched and took a moment to fully wake up. In the living room there were two couches facing a large flat screen television and a coffee table that sat on top of a cream colored carpet. There was no cable available but a Blu-Ray player was hooked up with a small pile of movies sitting next to it. In the far corner just after the television was the radio they used to contact Charlie Tippet. Jacob passed through the living room and into the kitchen where the front screen door Dawson had just come in and out of was located. Slipping into a pair of flip flops Jacob pushed the screen door open and stepped outside squinting into the sun. Although it wasn't even past seven in the morning the air was already warm.

"Dawson? Where are you?" Jacob called out.

"Over here, Daddy!"

Jacob turned, cupping his hand over his eyes against the glare of the sun and immediately felt a strong shiver run through his body. Sitting on the beach was the *Rose-Marie*.

The paint scheme of the *Rose-Marie* had originally been white but now it was quite faded with large deposits of rust on it from many years of neglect. The keel had dug into the beach a few inches and the boat was tilting to its port. It was over a hundred feet long and roughly twenty five feet wide with an aft deckhouse. The radar sat motionless on top of the deckhouse and the boat itself seemed to be dead. There was no sign of life or activity of any kind and it gave Jacob a feeling of uneasiness.

"It found us, Daddy!" Dawson was standing off the port bow looking back at his father. "We didn't even have to look for it!" He looked up at the ship. "I can't wait to see what's inside!"

"Dawson! Get away from there!" Jacob started to run towards his son yet never took his eyes off of the ship. Dawson pulled his hand away from the *Rose-Marie* and looked at Jacob with disappointment. "Come on, son, it's not stable enough to stand around." Jacob put his arm around Dawson and started to lead him away.

"How do you think it found us, Daddy?"

Jacob looked at the words *Rose-Marie* painted on the hull and noticed that rust surrounded the letters yet never touched them. It was as if the name had to remain clear and readable with no blemishes.

They went back inside the cottage but before the screen door closed, Jacob threw a quick glance back at it.

It found us.

***

Emily came out of the bedroom wearing a pair of short

shorts and a small tank top with her dirty blond hair still messy from a good night's sleep. She looked over at Dawson who was sitting at the small round table in the kitchen eating some cut up melon. He looked up from his pieces of fruit and smiled at his mother.

"What's going on?" Emily asked. She walked over and popped a piece of Dawson's melon into her mouth.

"Just having a snack while Daddy tries to call the Coast Guard."

Emily frowned slightly, "Why's Daddy trying to call the Coast Guard?"

"The ghost ship found us," Dawson said. "It's on the beach."

"Piece of shit!" Jacob tossed the radio's microphone in frustration.

"Daddy swore," Dawson said.

"I noticed," Emily said shooting Jacob a dirty look.

"I can't raise anyone," Jacob said. "Not Charlie Tippet, not the Coast Guard, nobody."

"Did you try the satellite phone?" Emily asked taking another piece of melon.

"First thing I did," Jacob replied, "I can't get a signal. It's almost as if…"

Emily looked at him, "As if what?"

Jacob looked down at his feet, feeling a little silly about what he was going to say, then met his wife's gaze, "It's as if something is blocking the signal."

"Blocking? What do you mean blocking?"

"I mean preventing us from being able to reach anyone, like our communications have been cut." Jacob said.

"And who would be blocking us?" Emily asked.

"The *Rose-Marie*!" Dawson said excitedly. "Come and see!"

He jumped down from the chair, grabbed Emily's hand and started to lead her outside.

"Slow down there buster," Emily laughed.

Like Jacob, Emily found the sun bright and cupped her hand over her eyes. She stopped dead in her tracks and felt her mouth fall open as her eyes locked onto the *Rose-Marie*.

"Isn't it cool?" Dawson asked. He broke free from Emily's hand and ran a little bit closer to it but kept his distance.

"It's… it's…" Emily tried to find the right words but couldn't.

Jacob stepped out behind her and put his hands on her shoulders.

"I was hoping to reach the Coast Guard or Charlie so someone could come out and deal with it," Jacob said.

Emily lowered her voice, "Do you think anyone's on board?"

"I haven't seen any indication of it," Jacob said.

They both stared at the ship in silence for a few minutes.

"Can we go on the ghost ship?" Dawson asked breaking the silence.

"No buddy, it's too dangerous." Jacob said.

"What if there's someone in there?" Dawson asked, scowling.

"There's not," Emily said, "it's just an empty…"

Her voice trailed off when she realized that there was a foreign noise in the air that wasn't native to the island and when she looked at Jacob, she could tell he could hear it too. They listened carefully and both came to the realization at the same time that the noise was coming from the *Rose-Marie*.

"What do you…?" Emily began to ask.

Jacob shushed her and as they listened the sound became more recognizable. It sounded like a man wailing in pain.

"Mommy," Dawson asked whispering, "is someone there?"

"Oh Jesus," Emily gasped, "someone *is* on board."

Jacob swallowed hard and took a few steps towards the *Rose-Marie* while motioning for Dawson and Emily to stay back.

"*Hello?*" he yelled out. "*Hello? Can anyone hear me?*"

He looked back at his family and saw that Dawson was biting down on his bottom lip. His eyes were wide with fear and he was inching closer to Emily. Dawson hugged her leg and she put her hand on his head.

"Take him inside," Jacob said. "Try to get ahold of

somebody… *anybody*."

Emily nodded and started to guide Dawson back towards the cottage. Once he saw that they were back inside, Jacob took off running behind the cottage and headed for the unfinished shed in the backyard. Lying beside it partially covered in tall weeds was his ladder. He wiped some spider webs off of it as best he could before he picked it up and ran awkwardly back towards the *Rose-Marie*. As he approached the ship the uneasiness he felt when he first saw it came back. He stopped just short of it and thought about turning around when the wailing became louder.

It was definitely coming from inside the *Rose-Marie*.

Jacob placed the ladder down in the sand and extended it as far as it would go. Struggling, he picked it up and carefully made his way to the starboard bow. He stood the ladder up and then tried to ease it against the *Rose-Marie* but it slipped and it smacked into the side. It echoed deeply in the ship and Jacob held his breath almost sure that the ship would roll on its side but it held. The ladder barely reached the railing but it was tall enough for him to climb on board.

"*Hey! I'm climbing up the starboard side! If you can hear me stay where you are!*"

He steadied the ladder as best he could in the sand and then slowly started to climb up the ladder one rung at a time. For some weird reason as he approached the railing Jacob became aware that his fear of the ocean was growing inside him. The tide was low and the *Rose-Marie* wasn't even in an inch of water but he felt very anxious about the ocean nonetheless. Something was wrong but he couldn't quite put his finger on it. When he reached the top of the ladder, Jacob grabbed a hold of the railing and began to pull himself over onto the deck.

The ladder suddenly began to slide to the right along the hull and Jacob frantically mustered his strength to complete his climb over the railing. No sooner had he landed on the deck when he heard the ladder fall away from the *Rose-Marie* and thud back down on the beach. Jacob stood up slowly and peered over the railing down at his ladder below.

"Shit."

Jacob was standing on the forward section of the deck amongst some old fishing equipment. Some of it was still neatly stowed away but most of it was strewn about the deck most likely as a result of the vessel's journey across the Pacific Ocean with no one at the helm. There was an opening in the middeck that led to what Jacob believed to be the holding tanks. As he made his way along the deck he found it slick and when he peered inside the tanks he found them empty.

Who was on board?

The wailing suddenly became frantic and desperate. Jacob cupped his hands over his mouth and yelled, "*Stay where you are! I'm coming!*"

He ran as fast and as cautiously as he could towards the deckhouse. The hatch leading into it was slightly ajar thanks to the angle the ship was sitting at and Jacob managed to slip inside.

It was dark inside the *Rose-Marie* and Jacob found he was standing in a small room where rain pants and jackets were hanging on either side from rusted hooks, obviously not having been worn for some time. He made his way through the room and stepped through a hatch on the other side which led into a hallway.

There was a doorway on either side and in each room there were four bunks. Personal items and the blankets had been tossed around like someone had slept in them at some point but like the rain gear, not for some time. The air in the bedrooms smelled thick and stale. Half-torn posters hung on the walls and were yellowing at the edges. He sifted through some of the belongings looking for a picture but couldn't find any.

"Hello? Can you hear me?" Jacob called out. "Anyone?"

The wailing had ceased but Jacob's interest in the *Rose-Marie* had grown, so he ventured on from the crew quarters.

At the end of the hallway was a hatch that led into the dining room and kitchen. A small round table with a circular bench around it was bolted down immediately to the door's left. There were a couple of plates and utensils still sitting on it but most were on the floor. When he stepped inside he immediately gagged. Rotten and spoiled food had been plastered everywhere; on the floor, the walls and the ceiling, giving off an odor that was similar to bile. Somewhere inside that thick, nauseating aroma, Jacob thought he could detect a metallic taste of blood. Although he felt like he would throw up at any moment, he searched through some of the rot looking for any evidence that a crew had recently been here. He found none.

A hatch at the far end of the kitchen gave way to a set of steep stairs that led up to the bridge. As he got closer to the steps the smell of blood became more pungent. His hands were shaking as he placed them on the wooden hand rails on either side of the stairs. In his mind he could picture the bridge as the place where all the bodies would be. He could see bodies with throats ripped about, stomachs torn open and limbs torn off of torsos.

"Get a fucking grip," Jacob muttered. His voice sounded loud in the deathly quiet ship.

When he reached the top, he stepped onto the bridge.

The main windows that looked out onto the deck were coated with a thick layer of grime. Modern navigational equipment had been set up but the power had long since been lost and all of the screens were black. Old navigational and fishing charts still hung on the wall but were quite faded and when he tried to read them to get an indication of where the ship had been, he couldn't as all of the writing was in another language. Jacob's eyes continued to roam around the bridge until they locked upon the skeletal remains of two men. One was seated in the captain's chair at the wheel and had on a pair of faded jeans with a tattered shirt with "Rose-Marie" stenciled on over the left breast. There was a large hole in the back of his head.

On the floor behind him was another skeleton but it looked fresher somehow, like it wasn't as old as the captain. It only had on a pair of cut off jean shorts. Most of the skin had peeled off of the body over time but the scalp was still more or less intact except for a hole that had exploded from the inside out. Dried blood and gore decorated the floor as well as the wall. Jacob felt as if he was about to gag but managed to keep the contents in his stomach down.

A Colt Python revolver was clutched in the right hand of the second body.

Both men had taken their own lives.

Jacob just stared at the two bodies wondering what had made them commit suicide. He also began to wonder where the rest of the crew was. Knowing there was still the engine room to check, Jacob was about to leave the bridge when suddenly the floor beneath him became unstable and the *Rose-Marie* began to rock violently back and forth. His arms flailed, frantically trying to grab onto anything but he lost his balance and fell forward, striking his head on the edge of the wheel in front of the dead captain.

***

Like Jacob had done earlier, Emily threw the radio's microphone in frustration after trying to reach Charlie Tippet and the Coast Guard. She couldn't tell if her calls were even going out as all she got as a response was static. The satellite phone was lying face down on one of the couches after failed attempts to even get a signal. She felt a slight hint of panic as for the first time she truly felt cut off from the rest of the world.

"Son of a bitch..." She muttered. Sighing heavily she looked over at Dawson who was sitting at the small table in the kitchen.

"Mommy, what's a son of a bitch?" Dawson asked.

"It's nothing big guy," Emily said. "It's just a phrase grown-ups use when they're frustrated and have nothing else to say."

Dawson nodded but didn't really understand what she meant and so he hopped down off of his chair. He walked over to the window and looked out at the *Rose-Marie*. All of the excitement he had felt when the ghost ship had first beached itself outside their cottage was gone and had been replaced by fear.

"Do you think Daddy's okay?"

"I'm sure he is, honey," Emily replied running her hands through her hair.

"I don't like him being on it," Dawson said.

Sensing that he was close to crying, Emily said, "I don't either but your dad's a tough and strong man. Strongest that I know. Otherwise I wouldn't have married him. He'll be okay." She walked over and hugged him. "Plus he's helping whoever that is on the ship."

"Mommy, what if it's the ghosts?" Dawson asked. "What if the ship wants his soul?"

A quiet rumbling made itself known and as Emily looked up to see where it was coming from, it suddenly erupted into a deafening roar. She barely registered what was happening when the cottage began to shake violently. The windows rattled, cracked, and then shattered all in the span of a second. Dawson began crying hard and was screaming. She scooped him up and ran for the bedroom doorway. Dishes and glasses fell from the cupboards, smashing onto the kitchen floor.

"It's okay Dawson! I got you!" Emily yelled. "Everything's going to be okay!"

Standing in the doorway feeling like the earth was trying to rip the cottage out of its surface, Emily had a hard time believing her own words. The cottage creaked and groaned as it was placed under incredible stress.

Just as suddenly as it started the shaking stopped and all was silent except for Dawson's sobs. Emily stayed in the doorframe and stroked his hair calming him down. Her eyes strayed to one of the shattered windows and outside she could see the *Rose-Marie* leaning on its starboard side.

"Jacob!"

She started to walk slowly toward the front door, where Dawson squirmed and she put him down. They both started to make their way cautiously towards the *Rose-Marie*.

***

Jacob's eyes slowly opened but all he could see at first was a blur. They slowly came into focus and he was staring at the skeletal feet belonging to the captain and it brought him back in a hurry. He pushed himself up onto his hands and knees while scurrying away backwards. Warm blood was slowly running down his face from a laceration to his scalp. When his feet hit the wall he managed to get to his feet but the floor felt different.

The *Rose-Marie* was no longer leaning to port.

What the hell happened? He thought.

From somewhere outside he could hear a voice calling his name. He wiped some of the grime off of the nearest window and peered out. Emily and Dawson were heading towards the *Rose-Marie*. A brief smile of relief broke on his face at the sight of them but almost as soon as it did a wave of nausea hit him. Sudden and strong panic ran through him.

Jacob turned around and made his way down the stairs into the kitchen and dining room as fast as he could. It was even more of a mess thanks to the earthquake and the smell of rot had gotten stronger. Jacob dry heaved but kept going, putting the back of his right hand under his nose to try to block the smell.

He rushed past the rain gear with his arm brushing against some of the sleeves. His foot caught the bottom of the hatch and he spilled onto the deck striking his knee hard. The pain was excruciating but he did not stop to nurse it. Deep in the pit of his stomach he felt that the worst was yet to come. He needed to reach his family. *Something was about to happen*.

"Emily!" Jacob yelled.

He hobbled over to the railing and grabbed on, careful not to fall over as the boat was now resting on its starboard side. His wife and son were standing at fallen ladder.

"Are you okay?" Emily asked.

"Shaken and sore but otherwise I'm fine." He looked at Dawson. "What about you, champ?"

"Just come off the boat, Daddy. Please." Dawson was on the verge of crying again.

Emily squatted down and started to lift the ladder. As Jacob watched her maneuver the ladder into its vertical position he could not shake the feeling in his gut. Emily struggled with it and lost her grip. She jumped back as the ladder hit the sand and she swore under her breath.

"Take your time, babe. It's awkward but you can do it." Jacob said.

"I think it was an earthquake," Emily said. "British Columbia was long overdue I suppose." She hoisted the ladder up again and it clanged against the side of the *Rose-*

Marie.

"Hey, Mommy, look!" Dawson suddenly said.

He took off running towards the water. Jacob and Emily both watched him, not understanding what he was seeing. Emily released her grip on the ladder and it slid off of the *Rose-Marie*. Jacob still didn't understand until he heard it.

It immediately pierced his stomach and freed the deep feeling of dread.

It was the sucking sound!

"Dawson! Come back here!" Jacob panicked.

"The water's going away!" Dawson cried out.

He was quite far from the aft of the *Rose-Marie*. Emily was running after him knowing full well what was going on. Jacob felt tears running down his face.

It was coming.

The earthquake had triggered a tsunami.

"Emily! Get him! For the love of God, get him!"

The sucking sound had ceased and Jacob had to lean over the railing to see where his wife and son were. She had reached Dawson and was trying to pick him up but he was putting up quite the resistance. In the silence Jacob could hear her talking to Dawson.

"Dawson, come on honey, we have to go." Emily could not hide the fear in her voice. "We have to go now."

"But Mommy, what's that?" Dawson asked. He was pointing out towards the ocean where a giant wave was racing towards them. It looked small in the distance but was closing in. Fast.

"Run!"

Jacob tried to climb over the railing but the *Rose-Marie* suddenly shifted back towards port and he fell onto the deck knocking the wind out of him.

"No... no... no..." he moaned as he struggled to get back up.

He could hear the rumbling now. It sounded exactly like it did in his dream: like a train racing down the tracks. Jacob got to his knees and grabbed the railing to help pull him up. He had to reach them.

Emily had gotten Dawson into her arms and was running back towards the beach.

She was running fast, but not fast enough.

The tidal wave was bearing down on them like a predator chasing its prey.

In a last ditch effort to climb over the railing, Jacob pulled with all his strength but he lost his grip as if the ship was preventing him from joining his family. He smacked his chin on the bottom rung of the railing, biting down hard on his tongue.

Just like in his dream, he could not reach his family.

He looked down upon his wife and son for the last time with the last expression on their faces was of complete and utter terror.

Jacob felt the wave slam violently into the *Rose-Marie*

resulting in a hard shudder, just as it rushed over his wife and son. He howled but the deafening roar of wave drowned out his cries. The ship was dislodged from the beach and pushed inland with the wave. Jacob held on the bottom rung as best he could but he was sent sprawling along the deck as the ship was at the mercy of nature. He was tossed around like a piece of debris in the wave's powerful grasp but quickly found himself near the hatch into the deckhouse. Survival mode took over and he wrestled his way inside.

Any form of rational thought was gone as the image of his family being swept up by the large tidal wave haunted him. It kept replaying in his head over and over again as he fought his way through the crew quarters and into the dining room. The smell of rot didn't register with his senses as he felt completely numb by watching the demise of his wife and child. He was unaware that his voice had become raw from his agonizing howls and darted up the stairs leading up to the bridge.

The captain had been thrown out of his chair and the other skeleton had slid to the other side of the bridge. Jacob didn't even bother stealing a glance out of the window. He knelt down beside the second skeleton and pried the Colt Python out of the boney fingers.

He checked the cylinder and there were four bullets left inside.

Jacob remembered telling his wife that he was not going to let his fear of the water affect their lives.

The barrel was cold as he slid it into his mouth.

He thought of his son sitting by the fire the night before with marshmallow sticking on his face.

His thumb pulled the hammer back.

He thought of his wife lying naked in the sand after they had made love.

His index finger applied pressure to the trigger.

After a loud bang, the *Rose-Marie* was once again without a living soul on board.

As the dead ship drifted out deeper into the Pacific Ocean it began practicing its wails. The voice it was mimicking was Jacob's.

Pool Closed

Shenoa Carroll-Bradd

A knock sounded on the door to the manager's office of The Comfort Inn hotel, and at first, Harvey Nein pretended not to be in.

"Mr. Nein?" Sylvia's soft voice came through the particle board. "Jimmy said he saw it again last week."

Harvey sighed. "Did you tell him no one's falling for that?"

Sylvia opened the door a foot, just enough to look at him. No, she hadn't, he could see. She was far too shy for that.

He rubbed his jaw. "Have *you* seen anything?"

She shook her head, eyes on the worn brown carpet.

"Fine. Just tell him to...make a note of it, if he wants, and get on with his work."

She nodded, and began to back out of the office, eyes still down, when the walkie-talkie at her hip bleeped a herald.

"Front desk, come in, over," came Jimmy's crackling voice.

She lifted the radio, giving Harvey an apologetic look. "Yeah, I'm here. Over."

Harvey rolled his eyes and waved at her to close the door on her way out.

She grabbed for the doorknob and had the door halfway closed when the walkie-talkie crackled again.

"Come down to the pool," Jimmy said, his voice unsteady beyond the static. "You've gotta see this."

The door slowly swung in again, and her dark eyes rose to meet Harvey's gaze.

"It's back." Jimmy finished. "Over."

"I'm going to fire him, I really will this time," Harvey said as he rose from his chair. "You stay up here. Man the desk."

Sylvia nodded and ducked behind her counter.

***

James does passable janitorial work, can't be faulted there, Harvey thought as he strode down the hotel corridor. *He doesn't show up to work drunk or stoned, but there has to be a rule somewhere in the employee handbook that warns against crying wolf.* If there wasn't, Harvey was going to add one.

He pushed open the doors to the indoor pool and glared.

James stood in the far corner, his back almost against the wall.

"Well?" Harvey demanded. "What's so important that I just *have* to see it?"

James looked up at his boss, then extended one arm toward the pool that sparkled like a rippling gem between them. No matter his other faults, James certainly kept a clean pool.

Harvey followed the janitor's shaking finger down to the water, and his breath caught. He saw it too, moving like a torpedo though the water. He took an involuntary step back. "That's...that's not..."

"It is, though."

"That's not possible."

"No," the janitor agreed. Neither man moved as they watched the shadow circle for another few seconds.

"How did it get in?" Harvey muttered. "How is it...breathing?"

"I dunno."

"How many times have you seen it now?"

"Four. I didn't tell nobody the first time, because I didn't even believe it myself. But you see it too."

"Yes," Harvey breathed, "Yes, I see it too. I used to have...nightmares, just like this when I was little. I would cry whenever my mom took me to swim lessons."

James hefted a long pool skimmer and stepped closer to the edge.

"What are you doing?"

"Just testing." James turned the skimmer around and leaned over, jabbing the long pole into the water. It connected with the circling shape and passed right through without disturbing their visitor.

Harvey stepped closer. "So it's not real? We're just...hallucinating. Just a group delusion, caused by," he looked around the enclosure, "stress, or exposure to chemicals, or..."

James shook his head. "It doesn't stay long." He replaced the pool skimmer on the rack. "Starts as a shimmer, and then just fades away when it's ready to leave." He walked over to a shape hidden under a tarp in the far corner by the pumps. "But for the brief time it's here," he flipped back the cover, "it's *really* here."

Harvey walked around the edge of the pool, keeping his distance and checking over his shoulder every few steps, then came to a stop before James' evidence. Under the tarp lay the jagged remains of the pool-cleaning robot, its tubes severed, its plastic case fragmented and split. Harvey stared at it for a moment. "When did this happen?"

"Found it this morning. Hauled it out about an hour ago." He glanced at the shadow in the pool, dimmer now, less defined. "I think it's attracted by movement."

Harvey's posture tightened, and he drew himself upright. "Seal it up," he said. "No one comes in here, not even to clean. Not until we figure out what the hell is going on."

James nodded and pulled the tarp back over the robot wreckage. "Want me to drain it first?"

Harvey glanced back at the pool. The water was bright, blue, inviting. The pool looked beautiful, and entirely empty. He shivered. "No. I don't think that would make any difference, and it might draw some...undue attention." He shook his head firmly. "Lock it up and let's go."

Three weeks later

The boys were being obnoxious. They played full-contact punch buggy, and if the highway ran low on VW beetles for any length of time, they began to hit each other for Mustangs, trucks... and eventually anything with wheels.

Leslie wouldn't have minded if they were both hers, but the younger boy was her sister's tax break and, for the weekend, her headache. He was a smart little shit, that Robert. Her own boy wasn't anything special in the brains department, but he had muscular legs and an unusually high pain tolerance that made him the apple of every coach's eye. College was still a long way off, but the way things were headed, he was only going on a sports scholarship. Her Joey was a good boy at heart, just a little dumb.

She'd agreed to take Robert for the weekend, while her sister Sarah was at her big important user's conference. She never missed an opportunity to rub Leslie's nose in the fact that she managed to have a career *and* a kid. As if being a mother weren't enough.

So, there they were, headed to Sea World San Antonio. Robert read a lot of nature books about the ocean, and Joey... well Joey liked movement and bright colors.

***

An hour later, they pulled into the crumbling asphalt parking lot of The Comfort Inn hotel.

Leslie frowned. "This place looks like a-" she stopped herself, aware that both boys' ears had perked up. Preteen boys seemed to have impending swear radar. "Dump," she finished carefully, though Joey still snickered.

"You said find cheap accommodations," her husband Mark replied, turning off the car. "So I did. I dare you to find anything cheaper."

Leslie didn't want to take that bet. To its credit, The Comfort Inn wasn't just a string of motel hovels, it was a proper hotel building, all internalized.

"I'm going to check us in," Mark said. "Why don't you and the boys grab our bags?"

The sun was already hitting Leslie hard. She could feel a migraine building. "Sure. Fine." By the time she got the boys out of the car, made them stop running each other's feet over with the luggage, and brought them all inside, Mark had completed their booking.

A mousy, skittish looking clerk was just handing him the key cards. "And there you are, room 313. Elevators are just down the hall to your left." She turned a timid, forced smile on the rest of them, as if children made her nervous.

Smart girl. She saw Joey whispering to his cousin as they approached the elevators, but couldn't make out any words.

Robert shook his head, but Joey laughed. It wasn't until the doors closed that she realized what her darling son, light of her life, had been planning. He let loose a fart like a trumpet blast before doubling over with joy at the disgusted reactions of his captive audience. Mark slapped him, lightly, on the back of the head, and Joey suddenly didn't think it was so funny anymore. The four of them burst out of the elevator when it opened, and walked down the quiet, carpeted hall to their room.

Leslie's head felt like it was building pressure, swelling and throbbing. She touched Mark's arm when he unlocked their room. "I'm gonna need to lie down for a bit."

He frowned and kissed the top of her head. "Aw, sorry hon. Migraines again?"

She nodded. "Started right when we pulled in. Do you think you can keep the boys quiet until my pill kicks in?" She followed his gaze to the double beds, where Joey and his cousin were already pulling off the blankets to make a tent.

"I'll do my best."

***

Ten minutes later, Joey stood with his nose pressed to the window, watching traffic like a dog left in the car while his owner shopped.

Robert sat on the floor beside him, reading a book about oceans. "Did you know that about 100 million years ago, in the Cretaceous Period, this was all underwater? The whole of Texas."

"Uh huh," Mark said. He'd already kicked off his shoes and was watching a hockey game on mute.

Leslie said nothing. She'd taken her pill but it hadn't kicked in yet, so she was lying on the bed with a pillow over her face. There was nowhere she could go to escape the light and chatter of the boys unless she curled up in the bathtub, but with three guys sharing the room, she knew it wouldn't be long before someone interrupted.

"Slug bug," Joey said, followed by a pained grunt from his cousin.

"Is there a quieter game you two can play?" she asked. "Out in the hall, maybe? I just need some peace, please."

She heard footsteps, too small to be Joey's, then a little voice from over by the door. "Hey, this place has an indoor pool. Can we go swimming?"

"Yeah, can we?" Joey joined in. "We've got our suits and everything."

"That's weird." Mark shifted beside her. "The desk clerk didn't mention a pool. Usually cheap places like this never shut up about their amenities."

Leslie kept the pillow over her face. "Fine. Yes, go swimming. Just stop talking about it, please."

The boys whooped, then remembered her state and noisily hushed each other.

She heard their footsteps clomping back and forth as they got out their suits and took turns getting changed in the bathroom. "You go with them," she murmured to Mark.

"Shh. Just relax." He patted her hip.

Leslie forced herself to focus on the darkness behind her eyes until the commotion of the boys gradually faded away, replaced with quiet, soothing serenity.

***

Joey and Robbie tramped down the carpeted hallway to the elevators, slapping their plastic flip-flops as hard as they could against the soles of their feet, trying to see whose was louder. Robbie's towel covered his narrow shoulders like a cape, held together at his throat with one fist, while Joey draped his across the back of his neck and pulled the middle up like a hood. Joey pranced as they entered the elevator, declaring shrilly, "I'm a Lay-day, dah-ling." He hit the button for the lobby.

"The map on our door said the pool is down the hall from the lobby," Robbie explained. "So when we get to the bottom, we just keep going straight down that way."

"Beautiful, dah-ling. Straight down the runway."

"I'd rather taxi down the runway," Robbie declared, pulling his cape out into wings and swerving in the small space, making a noise like machine gun fire with his mouth.

Joey switched into a fighter plane as well, and they had a death-defying three second dogfight before the elevator came to a stop.

Robbie grabbed hold of his cousin as soon as they stepped out. "Bet we're not supposed to be down here by ourselves." He brought a finger up to his lips and stepped out of his flip-flops.

Joey did the same, then the pair tiptoed down the hall, past the front desk. They stopped outside the pool and stared at the chain running through the handles and the poster board sign taped across the doors. "Pool Closed," it declared in thick, black sharpie letters.

"Lame!" Joey's shoulders slumped beneath his brightly colored towel.

Robbie cupped his hands and pressed his face to the

frosted glass strips to either side of the doors. "It's dark, but it looks like there's still water in the pool." He took his hands away. "If it was really closed, they would have drained it, right?"

Joey shrugged. "Maybe they just say it's closed during the day to keep kids out, and then all the adults go and swim naked at night."

Robbie pulled a face. "Gross, dude. I don't want to swim in the same pool as naked old ladies."

"Doesn't matter anyway." Joey lifted the rectangular combination lock holding the chain together and let it drop again, like the knocker on an old haunted house.

"Maybe not. Give me a second." Robbie picked up the combination lock and began fiddling with it, turning his back to his cousin.

"Well, if we can't get in, then we'll go find something else. I bet they've got an ice machine somewhere. We could have a cube fight."

Something clicked and Robbie turned back, the open lock in his hand, a wide smile on his face. "I got it."

"Holy-" his cousin's eyes went wide. "Look at you, secret bad-ass!"

Robbie shrugged. "I just guessed lucky. 1-2-3-4. It's the laziest combination in existence. My mom uses it for all her passwords."

They pulled down the sign, opened the door and slipped inside.

The water level was a little low in the pool, a few inches

of painted plaster stuck up along the sides, but the water was clear, and the air stung with chlorine. It seemed strange to have the pool all to themselves; the slap of their feet and the echoing ring of their voices made the whole thing seem secret and naughty.

"Dip in a toe, see how cold it is," Joey dared.

"No way. You do it."

Joey turned and gave him a hard look. "Don't tell me you're scared of water, you big baby."

"I'm not," Robbie shot back.

"Yes you are!" his cousin crowed, dropping his towel and flip-flops by a lounge chair. "You're scared of a stupid old swimming pool!"

"Shut up! No I'm not." Robbie ditched his belongings beside his cousin's and went to the lip of the pool. "Just watch." He stuck one leg out, inching his toe toward the water's crisp aqua surface.

Joey planted both hands on Robbie's back and shoved him in.

Robbie flailed as he hit the pool, chlorine-tinged water shooting up his nose as he sank. He heard the percussive impact as Joey cannon-balled in after him. Robbie fought his way up to the surface and spat out a mouthful of pool water, glaring at his cousin, whose wet hair hung down over his face like a sheepdog's.

When he saw his cousin's expression, Joey spiked a wall of water at him.

Robbie splashed back, and they carried on a war of

waves and teasing threats until one of Joey's barrages hit him straight in the eyes. He spun away from the attack, ducking his head and swiping at his face, trying to clear his stinging vision. Something passed through the water a few feet from his hip, a broad grey torpedo, circling left. His head snapped up. The hotel pool glistened teal all around them, empty but for the islands of their bodies.

Joey stared at him. "You okay, dude? I didn't mean to get you in the eyes like that."

Robbie swayed to see around his big cousin, checking the shadows at the deep end of the pool. "Did you see that?"

Joey glanced over his shoulder for just a second before turning back. "All I saw was you losing. Loser." He swam to the side and hauled himself up out of the water.

"What are you doing?"

"Going on the diving board, what's it look like?" Joey's feet hit the cement with fat wet slaps.

"No," Robbie hissed. "What if someone hears you? They'll kick us out!"

Joey scoffed and waved a hand at him, not slowing.

Robbie scowled at the turquoise water by his cousin's pattering feet. There was something wrong with his reflection. The dim light coming in through the frosted glass walls created an odd glare on the water, he decided. That's what made it look like his cousin had a huge shadow.

***

Upstairs, Leslie stirred in her pillow sanctuary, where the air had grown too stuffy and close. She squeezed her eyes tight and pulled the pillow away, gasping with pleasure at the cool touch of the hotel's air conditioning.

"Well welcome back, sleepyhead," Mark said from beside her. "How are you feeling?"

Leslie's eyes shot open, stinging at the sudden onslaught of light. The room was eerily quiet. "What are you doing here? Where are the boys?"

"Pool," Mark said nonchalantly. "Headed down there just after you fell asleep."

"How long ago was that?" She swung her legs over the side of the bed and stood. The room blinked out in a sudden rush of black and white static. Leslie sank back onto the edge of the mattress, gripping her head.

"Honey, you okay? Need me to get you something?" He smoothed a hand across her back.

She jerked away. "I can't believe you let them go down there by themselves. What if they got lost? What if they got..." she waved her hands, "kidnapped or something?" She stood up, and this time she was able to walk without getting light-headed. "Sarah will never let me hear the end of it if her precious little nerd scrapes his knee, or catches pink-eye from a hotel pool."

"I really think you're over-reacting. They're good boys; they'll look after each other..."

She found her shoes and yanked them on. "Neither of them knows CPR," she snapped. "So yeah, they'll be able to watch the other one drown. Great, thanks." She stormed over and hauled open the door.

"Les, come on." Mark still hadn't turned off the TV, or even reached for his shoes.

Leslie looked at her husband lying there on the hotel bed, remote balanced on his ever-expanding belly. "No Mark, don't get up. I'll take care of it, like always." As the door swung closed, she called back, "Great parenting!"

***

Joey steadied himself on the diving board, bouncing on the end to test its spring.

Robbie stayed far out of range, treading water. He'd learned the hard way that his cousin found it hilarious to try to land right on top of him, and that their combined weight was enough to drive him to the bottom of the pool. The first time Joey had done that, Robbie had thought he was going to die.

"I'm serious," he called in hushed tones, "Don't jump. We're going to get in trouble if they find us. Breaking and entering, dude."

Joey shook his head as he bounced, pumping his arms back and forth as if he intended to launch himself all the way over to where Robbie waited.

For a moment, it seemed as if the shadow beneath the board moved. Robbie stared at it, trying to reconcile what he knew to be possible and what he was seeing.

"Here I come," Joey warned, bending the board farther than it had gone before.

"No, Joey, don't! There's a-" he couldn't get the words out. It was too crazy.

The shadows were moving. An oblong shape detached

and turned a slow circle beneath the board. "There's a shark!" He cried at last, just as a grey triangle of flesh cut through the quiet aqua water.

***

Leslie muttered all the way down the hall and swore during the elevator ride, so she could get it all out and be calm once she reached the front desk.

The mousy clerk looked up and faked a smile. "Hi there, how can I help-"

"Did you see two little boys go by? About nine and eleven?" Leslie hovered a hand by her breasts, trying to estimate how tall Joey was now.

The clerk's mouth drew into a concentrated frown. "Not since you checked in, no. Are they missing?"

No, Leslie thought, *I left them safe in the room. I'm just here to test your memory.* She pulled in a breath. "Hopefully not. My wonderful husband, God bless him, thought they'd be fine going to the pool by themselves, and now I'm..."

The clerk's eyes went wide at the word pool. "Oh, they're not there. I'm sure they're not. The pool's closed. It's been closed for weeks."

Leslie pulled back. "Well if they're not at the pool, then where-?"

The clerk lifted a black walkie-talkie to her mouth. "Jimmy, come in. We're missing two boys, about nine and ten-"

"Eleven."

"I have the mother here, she says they went to the pool. Over."

The response crackled back. "Pool's closed. Over."

Leslie rolled her eyes. "Tell him to look around for them! Stop telling me the stupid pool's closed, and tell me where the boys are!"

The clerk kept her eyes down. "Jimmy, can you come assist in the search, please? I'm covering front desk. Over."

"On my way, over."

"No, I don't need that guy's help, just point me toward the pool. If they're not there, they're probably somewhere close by."

After a moment's evasion, the clerk gave her directions, and Leslie set off across the hotel.

***

Joey scoffed again. "Don't be stupid." He bounced one more time, then leaped.

Robbie felt spreading warmth in the water as his bladder let go, and the sleek grey shark surged up to snatch his cousin from the air.

Millions of years, he thought in a moment of detached shock, *and they've hardly changed at all.*

It hit the water sideways with a monumental splash that knocked Robbie backwards. He felt a scream catch tight in his chest, a squeezing scream that would neither release nor let him breathe. He spun and struck out for the ladder, flailing more than stroking his way to safety. He couldn't think about what had just happened, there'd be time for that later. For now, all that mattered was the gleaming chrome ladder waiting just a few yards away.

***

Leslie turned the last corner in time to see a sweaty, gangly man enter the hallway through a side door. Bright sunlight flooded in with him, and the smell of baking asphalt.

She raised a hand to her temple. "Are you Jimmy?"

The man tipped his baseball cap at her. "The same." His gaze took in the pool doors, the poster board lying on the ground, and his sweaty face tightened. "That's supposed to be locked," he said in an unsteady voice.

"Yes, so everyone keeps saying." Leslie reached for the handles.

***

Robbie swam hard, straining and reaching, until one spastic hand finally closed on a slick metal rung. He turned, eyes burning, to gauge where the shark was, and came face to snout with the charging beast. Robbie had the barest second to turn and slip between the ladder and pool wall. The giant, tapered head crashed into his makeshift shark-cage, denting it concave and puncturing the boy's stomach with a broken rung. The pain of impact knocked the wind out of him, spreading dark blood through the water like an ink stain.

The shark circled away and charged again, opening its massive jaws to encompass both boy and twisted metal. Four rows of teeth struck Robbie at once, tearing his sides to corded ribbon. Air exhausted and drowning in a cloud of red, Robbie sank to the bottom with his eyes half-closed, as if drifting off to sleep.

The shark swung around for one final pass.

***

"Ma'am, don't! No one is allowed in there, that's why it's supposed to be locked-"

Leslie hauled open the pool doors, ignoring the janitor's protests. "Joey? Robert? If you two are hiding from me, you are going to be in the deepest trouble of your lives-" She stopped a few feet from the pool, staring into the strange, purple-brown depths. "What the hell is wrong with your pool water?"

Behind her, the janitor unclipped the walkie-talkie from his belt.

"Joey?"

A shape moved through the water, circling away from her. It might have been one of the boys, she couldn't tell. The weird, beet-colored water made it too hard to see.

The janitor hooked her elbow and gently pulled her away from the pool edge. Leslie shot him a dirty look for touching her without permission, but he wasn't paying attention to her. His eyes were following some shadowed movement in the water. She turned and headed to the familiar pile of flip-flops and towels left between two of the lounge chairs.

"Front desk," she heard the janitor say into his walkie-talkie, "I need the manager sent to the pool right away. We're gonna have some unhappy customers in a minute. Over."

The Flood

Justin M. Ryan

The rain hadn't stopped for almost a month. Every morning Kayla sat on her porch while her father drank his coffee and smoked his cigarettes, both of them staring out at the murky expanse encroaching across their back yard.

"It's just a bit of water. Water never hurt anyone," her father said when Kayla admitted to being scared one morning. Overnight the water had climbed over the bottom step, completely enveloping the entire yard save for the tallest and most resilient weeds. She could still see the top of her jungle gym even though the slide and the swings had already been consumed. Rust climbed from the surface of the water, spreading across the metal frame like a rash.

"Water kills people," Kayla argued. "Go stick your head in it and see if it doesn't." She knew better than to sass but her father had a way of talking down to her that always inspired venom. Usually he snapped back but this morning he remained quiet. Kayla heard him stamping his cigarette out on the ash tray but she didn't dare look back.

"Don't talk to me like that," he said, his voice unusually calm and measured. After a silent moment he stood up, kicked the dirt off of his boots, and disappeared into the house. The screen door clanked shut behind him and then Kayla was all alone on the back porch with the rain and the swelling lake.

The reflection of the dreary, ashen sky shimmered like a desert mirage as the surface of the water was pummeled by millions of little rain drops. Like grass growing, Kayla couldn't watch the lake rise but she knew next time she looked that it would be just slightly higher. Eventually it would cover the second step, then the third and then it would swallow her whole house, all in slow motion.

The sound of the rain on the tin roof had become a constant companion. Sometimes it was just background noise, barely audible over her own breathing but other times the squall drowned out the television and the radio and anything else, demanding her attention like a pushy salesman at the door. When she sat alone in her room and listened, Kayla could swear she heard patterns in the metallic chatter, some rapid voice speaking to her in a foreign language. It grew to sound like a stunted sort of speech, skipping like a scratched disk.

Kayla sat on the porch for a moment longer before following her dad inside. She had hoped to play outside for the first time in a month today, even if it meant donning her yellow slicker and rain boots and jumping in puddles on the street, but it was coming down heavy today and she knew without even asking that her dad would forbid it. Another TV day. She bounced up the wooden stairs to her bedroom two at a time, kicking up dust behind her. Ever since her mother died last year things had been left mostly alone and, as Kayla came to learn, things left alone in the house tended to gather dust. If it kept on raining she might start gathering dust herself.

***

Kayla drifted off while watching cartoons, lulled to sleep by the gentle patter against her window until a crack of thunder jerked her awake. The house shuddered and a burst of light streaked outside, briefly illuminating her dim bedroom. Kayla's heart missed a beat but the panic subsided with the grumbling thunder. She laid her head back down but felt that her pillow was damp and warm. She checked her sheets and realized she'd been sweating. The vague memory of a nightmare lingered in her mind. Something about the lake, she knew, but the details were lost to the haze during her abrupt wake up call.

The sound of her father's cursing from downstairs suddenly drew her attention from the dream and Kayla found him near the back door, kicking a towel around a giant puddle of water. As she approached, he glared up at her.

"How about closing the door all the way when you come in? Do you see all this?" He growled, gesturing at the wooden floor. A pond had formed in the living room, starting at the back door, and had spread all the way into the laundry room and her father's bedroom. She watched the edge of the puddle as it slowly expanded, creeping towards the bottom of the staircase. A rush of fear filled her then, for her father's temper and for something else, some unexplainable dread.

"I'm sorry! I didn't mean to!"

Kayla's father crossed his arms and breathed in deeply, his nostrils flaring with barely controlled rage. He opened his mouth but snapped it shut and instead just pointed at the water with one hand and Kayla with the other. She ran down the stairs and started gathering towels, enough to soak up every bit of water that had come in. Her dad shook his head and left her to it, returning to his room and slamming the door.

Kayla spent the entire afternoon cleaning up the mess. It continued to spread even as she tried to control it and before long it had spread to the kitchen and the bathroom as well. She soaked every towel they owned, put them all in the drier for an hour, and then did it again until she was certain she had gotten every last drop. Satisfied, she set a second load on and headed back towards her bedroom.

As she was crossing the living room Kayla's feet slipped out from under her. She went over backwards, her thigh and shoulder taking most of the damage as she smacked into the hardwood floor. Pain flared through the entire right side of her body but she kept her teeth clinched to keep from screaming out and angering her father further. A cold wetness seeped through her sock and drenched her foot and she felt liquid sliding across her side.

Kayla clambered to her feet and investigated the wet spot that tripped her up and found a thin trail of water leading across the floor to the back door, a spot she had wiped up multiple times. She inspected the door and found the cause of the problem, a crack in the rubber seal on the bottom that was allowing the rain water through.

But if water can come in through that crack, then…

Kayla leapt to her feet and looked out of the window confirming her fear. The lake was no longer confined to the yard but had already overtaken the porch. Outside she saw nothing but standing water, the posts supporting the roof of the porch extending up from the ever growing quagmire. Kayla ran back to the dryer and pulled out all of the towels, mashing them up against the crack in the door to keep out the impending flood. She wanted to call her dad to help, since he'd know what to do, but she was scared he was still angry with her.

Kayla ran to the front door and looked out of the window, confirming the water hadn't reached up enough to block that exit. She breathed a sigh of relief when she saw her front yard sloping gently upward towards the road, lake free. She'd wait until he came out of his room and then they could evacuate. Kayla ran up the stairs to her bedroom, dragging her overnight bag out of the closet and scooping up all of her clean clothes.

The rain on the roof said her name.

When Kayla heard it she stopped what she was doing and froze, one ear cocked towards the ceiling. A steady bubbling as the rain gathered in the gutters, the repetitive, uneven tapping of individual drops on the tin. Nothing that formed a coherent noise, nothing that could, but still… she'd heard it. She knew she had. She started packing faster, emptying her drawers into the suitcase that was just slightly bigger than her. She grabbed her favorite toys and stuffed them into the side pockets before struggling to zip it all up over the bulges.

Look at me, the rain beckoned. Kayla shook her head to clear her mind and turned her ear to listen again. *Pitter patter… drip drop… plip plop. Nothing.* Kayla crossed her room to the window and swung open the curtains, her mouth dropping open when she saw the ocean her yard had become. The water formed a sheet over everything as far as she could see, only trees in the distance rising out of the grey-brown soup. The rain looked like static on a TV screen and filled the air with movement, a horde of translucent, silver wasps.

Kayla gaped for a long time at the swelling lake in stunned silence, its surface dancing with each drop. A shadow flitted across her vision then disappeared instantaneously, like a big fish exploring the shallows and retreating back into the depths. She wondered if there were a lot of fish in the lake now. Back when it was a pond, there were only a few but her father said when the water level got high enough it could reach other bodies of water and then everything in that water was in their pond too.

Maybe even alligators, Kayla thought, shivering. The black shape returned momentarily, swimming just below the surface, so faint in the cacophony of rain drops it might have just been a figment of her imagination. Kayla pulled the curtains closed and ran back down the stairs, her suitcase making a clunk on each step as she dragged it behind her.

The crack in the rubber had grown and water streamed in through the back door. Already the first floor was under water an inch deep. Kayla abandoned her suitcase on the stairway and kicked off her shoes, sloshing towards her father's closed door. She knew to knock but her adrenaline was pumping and she was too scared to be patient. She swung the door wide open and called for her dad. He was already awake, sitting on the edge of his bed with his feet in the water up to his ankles. He grasped at his head with both hands and he was weeping and wailing, though Kayla couldn't tell if it was sadness or anger or both. When she came in he jerked up, straightening his back and wiping his eyes.

"Kay?" He seemed surprised to see her.

"Are we going to evacuate?" Kayla asked, pleading with her eyes for him to say yes. He stood up and crossed the room, flicking the curtain to the side and peering out into the yard.

"No, honey... no point."

"But the water is really high!" Kayla argued, her voice growing shrill with panic. Her father kicked his foot up, splashing Kayla. The old man grinned and chuckled when Kayla withdrew. The sound was foreign to her and part of her wanted so bad to play this game with her dad, any game like they used to, but she couldn't. They had to leave.

"Dad..." She whined and his humor was gone then, replaced with a black anger. He trudged across the room and sat back on the bed, sneering.

"Go to bed, it will be fine in the morning."

Kayla felt her cheeks glow red with anger and she stomped her foot, forgetting she was in water and wasn't wearing any shoes. Her bare foot made a barely audible slap on the surface. Her dad snickered again and pulled a bottle of alcohol from his bedside drawer, screwing off the cap.

"I'm... really scared!" She admitted. Kayla was hesitant to show weakness again. It won her no points with her father, but she didn't know what else to do. He ignored her and poured the brown liquid into a little cup and drank the whole thing in one sip. Kayla sloshed over to the bottle, picked it up by the neck and slung it as hard as she could into the wall.

She expected a shatter of glass at least and hoped for a moment of lucidity from her father, some profound, immediate change, but the bottle just cracked through the plaster and left a huge hole in the wall. Completely undamaged, the glass bottle splashed into the water and floated in place. A split second later she felt hard, rough fingers wrap around her throat and she was slammed backwards onto the ground.

Kayla's head cracked into the floor and a wave of confusion washed over her. Her father squeezed her neck and held her still and even though she thrashed around all she managed to do was get her wet, stringy hair in her eyes so she couldn't see anything. She tried to apologize but his grip was too tight for her to speak. He was screaming but it sounded far away and muddled and she realized her ears were under water. She went completely still, her eyes clenched shut, and focused on drawing her tiny little breaths. She waited for him to hit her. He never had before, she never thought he would, but she knew now she was wrong. He would. Black spots swam across her vision as her father's grip grew tighter and tighter.

With fading consciousness Kayla's earlier nightmare came swimming back into her mind and she saw a lady in a bright red dress floating, suspended under water. The woman's hands reached for the dim promise of light above her but her feet disappeared into the blackness below, a silver cuff around her ankle kept her chained to the bottom. Kayla saw her from outside at first, like she was watching a television show, but then she was inside, seeing what the woman saw. She felt the water rushing all over her body, cascading around her and saw the light of day mere inches away, close enough to touch but not to breathe. Safety and warmth and all of reality was right there but it shimmered and shifted like a mirage and no matter how close she got, she wasn't there, she was stuck in the cold, in the dark.

The beating from her father never came and after a moment the grasp on her neck loosened, then released entirely. Kayla sat up, her head bursting out of the water and back into the light of day with a gasp. She scooted backwards into the wall, one hand going to her throat, the other brushing the tangle of hair out of her face as the water lapped at her chest and neck. The tears came then, heaving sobs made painful by the new soreness in her throat. Her vision was blurred but she could see her father standing on his bed, looking around wildly at everything but Kayla. He was shouting, long, wordless moans filled with anger and pain. Kayla pushed herself to her feet and was surprised to see how much water was in the room now as it came up to her waist.

The cascade of water in my nightmare. I was trapped and drowning.

Kayla shivered at the thought and looked towards her father's bed, where he had retreated. The posts on each corner stood like four islands in the brown, murky water that washed over the mattress and the pillows. Her dad stood in the center, the water almost to his knees.

"Do you see it?! Do you see it?!" Her father screamed, a drunken madman. Kayla lunged for the door, half wading, half swimming, focused only on escape. Once in the living room she saw that the back door had burst wide open allowing the water to gush in unconstrained, explaining the sudden flood. She shifted course for the front door, determined to leave with or without her father, but she saw then, drifting silently beneath the water, the same shadow she had seen from her window earlier. It looked larger now, sleek and skinny and it darted through the water with a grace like an Olympic swimmer. Panic seized Kayla and she darted for the stairway and the comfort of her own bedroom instead, kicking over her suitcase in the mad dash to get over it. She scrambled to the first landing, then turned back around when she heard a splash and scream. She saw the silent shape gliding just underneath the surface once again just before it disappeared into her father's room. Kayla tried to scream but her throat seized up and nothing escaped but a whimper.

Shh, child, the rain whispered, a comforting drone of noise. *You've nothing to fear,* it assured her. Kayla took the steps on her hands and knees, not trusting herself to run. Inside her room she slammed the door closed and locked it before dragging her chair under the handle. She considered barring the door with her desk but just then she heard another scream and stopped cold. From downstairs there came the sounds of thrashing and water churning, broken intermittently by her father's shouts of terror. The calls for help were choked and, as the seconds passed, grew weaker and rarer until finally all was silent again. Kayla collapsed against the door, sobbing.

***

Hours passed before she worked up the courage to open the door again and in that time the day gave way to night. From downstairs she heard a sudden series of popping noises a split second before the light in her bedroom shut off. A long, low buzzing noise slowly faded away and everything fell eerily silent. Kayla cracked open her door and peered out onto the first landing, where she saw water gently lapping at the steps. She stared at the surface for a long time, checking for any sign of the shadow even though she knew it was pointless. In the darkness, the water was pitch black ink.

A chill shot down Kayla's spine and the sensation of being watched prickled her skin. She spun around to look behind her but the room was as empty as it had been all day. She turned back to look at the water and screamed. A few feet away, at the very edge of the water near the stairs, a woman stared at her from the black abyss. Kayla slung the door shut and kicked away from it, scurrying on her butt into the center of her bedroom as she tried to come to grips with what she'd seen. Eyes. A woman's eyes, green like seaweed and long, yellow hair floating around her head like a crown. Kayla saw nothing more, for the woman stayed half underwater like a crocodile awaiting its prey, only the eyes above the surface and she only saw those because for just a second they caught the light and glowed like candles in the dark.

Kayla bolted for the window and scrambled to wrench it open. The sound of the rain filled the room, immediate and deafening. She climbed out onto her roof and surveyed the area around her, looking for something, anything that wasn't under water yet. The lake had completely covered the lower half of her house now and not even the top of her jungle gym or the roof of her porch were visible anymore. Kayla circled around the side of the house, clawing desperately at the slick tin for a handhold that wasn't there as the rain pounded around her, weighing her down and making every step more treacherous than the last.

The front yard, the front yard, the front yard. Kayla repeated in her head, a mantra to keep her sane as she inched her way across the roof. She didn't even make it halfway before her feet slipped from under her and she went sliding down the angled metal, the black lake rushing up to meet her.

She splashed into the abyss with a scream in her throat. The water rushed into her mouth and filled her lungs as she plunged downward. Kayla panicked when she didn't immediately surface and her writhing and twisting only disoriented her further until she didn't know which way to swim to get out. She picked a direction and lunged but as the water grew colder and darker, she knew she'd made the wrong choice. Despair settled in her stomach and the weight of it dragged her further into the black depths.

The woman came slowly, a black shadow growing lighter as she approached through the murky water. Her swim was inhuman, no arms or legs kicking, just her body bunching and curling like a snake as she sliced through the water, eerie and silent. On land Kayla could have run or fight or at least screamed but this wasn't Kayla's world. There was a threshold just a few feet above her head where everything changed. Down here she was slow, she was weak, and she was alone. She was helpless. There was no air for her to breathe, no noise, or even any light. A few feet, that's all it was. A few feet was the difference between land and water and it meant the difference between predator and prey, between life and death. Kayla screamed but no sound came out, nothing but a stream of bubbles that shot off to her left and disappeared.

Not to the left, she thought, *up.*

Kayla reoriented herself and kicked at the water furiously, confident she was rising towards the surface. She felt the distortion the raindrops caused all around her before she broke through the threshold and she began gasping at the air before she was even properly above water. She was still coughing when the hand wrapped around her ankle and dragged her back down into the depths. She kicked and struggled, swinging her fists but her attacks were stunted, weak, utterly ineffective. The woman pinned Kayla's arms to her side and stared into her eyes. That's when Kayla recognized her, the blonde, flowing hair, the shining green eyes; she was the woman from the nightmare. She was Kayla herself in thirty years. She was her *mother.*

Strong, sinewy arms wrapped around Kayla's shoulder like snakes and squeezed her so tight the air rushed from her lungs yet again. The embrace lasted less than a second and then the woman was gone, disappearing as swiftly and as silently as she had come, like a shadow fading into the night. Kayla resurfaced, gulping down air, and swam towards the front of the house until she felt the grass beneath her feet and the night air on her legs, then she collapsed.

The night felt empty somehow, too quiet, and Kayla realized it had stopped raining. She looked up at the sky and for the first time in a month she saw stars.

***

The lake receded as quickly as it rose but the house was beyond saving. Kayla moved in with her grandparents a few states away and stayed away from her childhood home for many years before she was able to return. Her nightmares never stopped but with the help of a therapist, she knew what they meant and why she had them. He helped her remember the night of her mother's death when Kayla stood at her window in her pajamas and watched her dad hold her mother underwater in the lake until she stopped struggling. Kayla had watched as he weighted her body down with chains and dropped her down to the bottom and she remembered the next morning when she went out to the water and saw, just beneath the surface, the shadow of her mother, a black shape with blonde hair billowing like a fan around her head. Her father had caught Kayla standing down by the lake that morning and he must have moved the body after that because the cops looked there. Kayla remembered that, she remembered thinking they'd find her there, but she'd made herself forget *why* she thought that. She'd made herself forget what she'd seen.

When Kayla's father went missing, the police searched the lake again and this time they did find her mother's corpse. She was clutching her husband's fresh body to her chest, her hands clasped around him, both of them drowned. It became an urban legend in Kayla's hometown, but everyone who knew the tale got one part wrong.

They thought it was a love story.

Crème Filling

Zachary O'Shea

Lindsey's hot tears eddied down rusted metal, pooled on the other side. They dripped into the fetid water below, rippled grimy surface. She tried not to cry. It wasn't easy with her face pressed hard enough against grating to bruise. Her life had fallen apart. She and her brother had been cast to the waves by the woman who'd promised to love them like a mother. "Too many greedy mouths to feed," she'd said. Father's scavenger ship had been away for months. Most assumed all hands were lost. Worst of all a Husk madly chanted on the other side of the door. She could hear the flesh-bag's footsteps scraping in the hallway as it searched for them.

"Tekeli-li. Tekeli-li." The hollowed woman repeated over and over, or rather the thing within her did. "Tekeli-li."

Her sibling kept his back flat to deteriorated door and knees against Lindsey's spine. There wasn't room enough for the both of them in this shambled alcove, but where else could they hide? Nate shallowly wheezed. The Husk was so close now. The saccharine scent its sort always exuded smothered the building's general stench of moist rot. Nate squeezed his eyes tight, losing a few tears of his own. The boy sucked in a breath, held it.

The unseen atrocity stopped droning, and then click-clicked with insect-like curiosity. Both children wanted to scream. They knew to do so would spell their doom. They'd be eaten from the inside out, worn like a suit of clothes.

An eyeless fish emerged from the filth on the other side of the grate. Its lips pecked against the water, the girl's tears mistaken for bugs skimming the surface. Without any prey the fish darted back into brackish depths. Lindsey stifled a hysterical giggle. Nate's knees pushed harder against her spine, a silent urge to be silent.

"Tekeli-li. Tekeli-li." The sound grew distant. In equal measure the pressure on Lindsey's backbone eased. She gulped in air and immediately started coughing. The water on the other side of the metal stirred, revealing the chewed-on cheekbone of a human skull just beneath.

"I need out." Her whisper dripped with terror.

Nate grunted. "Not yet. I want to make sure it's gone, Sis."

"Out." She riposted with a whine. A half-foot long amoeba lazily crawled out of the skull's mouth. Its clump-of-tar-like body was nearly translucent, displaying a lack of inner workings. Long mandibles manifested from its ropey flesh, dead-eyes floated along its back to stare at her. "Out."

"Lindsey."

"Slug." She squeaked and clamped her mouth shut as the six-inch invertebrate stretched for the source of warm breath. It managed to latch tiny cilia on the grating after spontaneously propagating the appendages. Dislocated eyes brimmed with malefic curiosity.

Throwing caution to the wind Nate slide the door aside, wincing as metal grated. He spilled into the hallway. She sprang away reflexively out the door, and sprawled across her brother's chest. Nate grunted in displeasure, rolled her off of him. He had the good sense to look down the dank hallway. On the other hand Lindsey gagged and felt frantically at her lips to make sure the putrid horror hadn't latched on.

"I want to go home." She shuddered.

"We don't have one." He reminded her as he got to his feet. There wasn't a time that Lindsey could recall Nate being anything but dour. His mood fit the world they'd been born into. "Let's get back to the boat and get out of here, okay?"

"Okay." She stood up, gripped his hand. "It's gone?"

"I think so. Come on."

The two fair-haired kids set off in the opposite direction from where the Husk went. They proceeded slowly through the piles of sodden debris, hanging fixtures, and collapsed floors. It didn't help that the sun was setting, the windows of the factory grimy. As they neared a hole where double doors used to hang Nate motioned for her to wait. He crept forward, curling as all children do when they were being sneaky. He wanted to make sure that they could dart past the gap without being spotted. So far they'd only come across one Husk, but there may be more skulking about. Somewhere nearby there could even be one of the primordial oozes which spawned the slugs.

While he scanned the processing floor, Lindsey studied the water-wrinkled posters on the walls. It was hard to imagine a time when children smiled and laughed as easily as portrayed. Each was in the process of eating a sugary treat, or begging a parent for one. One eroded advertisement in particular took the full brunt of the young woman's scrutiny: A child tugged on her mother's hand, stretching out far across a tiled hallway. She reached for a candy bar just out of reach, tongue poked out of mouth. The mother stood next to a cart with a can of vegetables in her other hand. She was looking down at her little girl, but sea water had ruined the ink and paper of the face. Her mouth was a gaping hole with distorted teeth and eyes little more than long slashes of black from brow to jaw line. Lindsey, despite her age, had seen things far worse than the twisted picture offered, but it still set her to quaking. What amazed her most about the advertisement were aisle shelves stocked with food. What bounty the world had before the caps melted, the seas rose, and long-frozen living sludge decimated what little remained of civilization.

"But Mom, I'm hungry now!" She whispered the sign's verbiage. Her thinned abdomen pulsed with desire. She'd forgotten how starved she was while fleeing for her life. Now it crept back in. "Is there any food?"

Nate curtly murmured as he turned back to her. "Huh? Who are you talking to?"

"Nothing. I'm just hungry." She listlessly gestured to some of the other placards where children their age smiled while gnawing on gingerbread men, clusters of nuts and chocolate, or rainbow-colored balls that apparently tasted like fruit.

"I know." Nate sighed. He motioned her closer while guilt crushed him. Their stale bread ran out yesterday and the half-submerged *Gingerbread House Candies Co.* factory had been too tempting to pass up. "I see some boxes from here. It might be food? Do we grab some, or head to the boat?"

She pulled on her chapped lower lip with a broken front tooth. "It's getting dark. We should get on the boat. I don't want to be in here in case there are any more Husks, you know?"

"Yeah. Okay, come on." He dashed across the aperture. She followed.

It wasn't long before they made it back to the stairwell, which stunk to high heaven. Salt-crusted concrete along with dead barnacles only added to the ambiance. They carefully made their way down a flight of rusty stairs, thankful for the open center so Nate could keep watch on the blind spot. The stairs kept going past the water line. They both fixedly watched the surface for any disturbance before heading through that floor's door.

In no time at all they retraced their steps through a hallway full of broken-down lockers and flotsam-laden rooms. This employee level of the factory had a balcony for workers to take smoke breaks on. It'd provided the perfect dock to tie a dingy too. Untended plants dominated the railing, and the world-wide ocean lapped over the edge. Their rubber boots splashed as they walked.

"Where… where is it?" Lindsey's voice trailed off into a high-pitched squeal. She stumbled forward and hopped up onto vine-infested barricade. "It's gone. Holy smokes! Nate!"

Dumfounded, the brother moved to the edge and hauled in the line still hanging there. He stared at the frayed end. "I… I…"

"There it is!" The sister pointed as she leaned far over the railing. Their rowboat rested against the corner of what was once a roof-top further down what used to be a city block. The setting sun lurked unseen behind the upper-stories of this once-bustling district. Its sanguine glow splashed across the ocean's surface, reflected off of rime-enameled windows, and bled through shattered facades. The dingy rolled with the current, bumping against pockmarked concrete. The boat wasn't moving, but was far out of reach. "There it is!"

"I see it. Keep your voice down, Sis." Nate resisted vomiting as anxiety clenched his stomach. All that was in there was acid and air; he didn't want either to come up. Without the boat they were doomed. He tossed the rope away and looked frantically around for something, anything that can aid them. With a snarl of frustration he tore off his ratty pea coat. "You stay here and be quiet. I'll go get it."

"No!" Fear bubbled up into a sob. Lindsey, despite being smaller than her sibling, hauled him upright. "No. The water is full of slugs, Nate. You can't swim in it. What if one gets in your mouth, or through your nose, or into your eyes? No. We'll just have to find another way."

"Lindsey. There is no other way."

His sullen tone didn't convince her. She wordlessly screamed as loud as she could. Her young body quaked violently, hands balling to fists. The shriek rolled like thunder off of drowned buildings. "Do you want to be a Husk too? Is that what you want? Because that's what's going to happen. You can't do that. You can't leave me! You can't! You can't!"

"I won't." He recoiled. Lindsey's hysterics almost broke Nate's composure. The balcony's rail held him up and he took in several long gulps of humid air. Below the water line, along sunken streets, a few street lamps eerily glowed as their timers activated. One sparked and then popped, dead forever. Nate tipped and looked down into the depths.

Lindsey was right; if he swam in that he'd end up dead one way or another. Clumps of toxic remnants drifted along, patches of oily scum too. A school of fish swam by, covered with malignant growths. The world of mankind was never meant to be underwater, centuries of industrialized sin steeped into a lethal concoction. He watched as a vast length of fleshy goo languidly slithered along the drowned avenue. The train-sized amoeba flowed over the twisted remains of a delivery truck. Now and again a fanged sucker would strike out, catch a passing fish, and drag it back into the mass. Eyes ranging from as big as a man to as small as a cat's roamed freely across the shoggoth's rippling surface. The impossible beast twisted and pushed through a curbside door. Its boneless bulk squeezed and shifted so it slid without difficulty. Soon the anathema was out of sight.

The idea of worm-like larvae from one of those things boring its way into his body numbed Nate when fear should have overruled his senses. Common wisdom held that the gargantuan protoplasms showed rudimentary, if alien, intelligence. Their sluggish spawn, on the other hand, loved to consume the insides of an earthly animal and wear it like clothing. Perhaps this newest generation craved something their blasphemous race never had-- a definable shape. Or perhaps this imitation had always been part of the abominations' lifecycle. Either way it didn't matter to Nate. He preferred not having all his insides eaten, his skin robbed.

He curled his hands around Lindsey's shoulders as she fell into muffled hiccupping. The dutiful brother considered wrapping his fingers around her small throat, sparing her what might come. She'd not seen the amoeba in the water below, didn't know the chance of escape was very slim. "Okay. You're right okay. Just breathe. We'll figure something out, Lindsey. Okay? We're going to be fine."

The fair-headed girl mutely nodded, leaned into the slow petting of her brother's hand. Despite their dire straits Lindsey didn't feel the crush of hopelessness that he did. She had absolute faith in Nate guiding her through this. He was second only to Papa.

"We good?"

His voice roused Lindsey from her thoughts, but she didn't cease clinging. "Yes. Do you think Papa will find us?"

He turned his face away, watching the dingy bounce around the corner it had been previously resting on. The rowboat all too soon drifted out of sight atop sanguine waves. Nate managed to keep his voice even. "I don't know, Lindsey. I hope so."

"But we left a trail for him to follow." She fiercely clutched to that hope as she did to her elder sibling. It had been Lindsey's clever idea to pilfer a box of digital markers days before they were finally cast to the pitiless sea. Even though the world had drowned, the junk shot into the heavens at civilization's pinnacle still spun silently. Thousands of satellites even now cavorted in orbit, and would continue their dance macabre for eons past humanity's extinction. Papa's crew used the ceramic spikes to designate salvage sites they wished to return to. He'd explained to his children once that each nail had a tiny computer inside of it which sent out signals to a network of satellites above. It had something to do with GPS, but neither child could remember that the letters stood for.

"I know."

Nate responded. Their step-mother erroneously thought he'd run away from her to try and hide like some coward, saw it as further proof she was doing the right thing by turning Nate and Lindsey out. In truth it was nothing more than a case of jealousy. Every time the harpy looked at the two blonde darlings all she could see was the ghost of the woman before her that needed to be exorcised. Nate used those stolen moments to shove the first of the markers in the secret spot where his father had hidden away artifacts that his current wife deemed as useless.

Every so often as the siblings drifted through the barely exposed spires of the sunken metropolis, they'd lance the side of a building with one of the white darts and activate it. The chances were slim that their sire was even still alive. When Nate considered the odds of Father understanding the significance of the marker, and then managing to follow them all, he promptly decided to stop considering them. No matter how strong and stoic Lindsey thought he was, he was still just a boy - a boy full of fear.

"Papa will find us. Everything would be okay."

Nate forced the words from his lips. "Everything will be okay."

One of the windows on their floor exploded in a rain of glass. An inhuman voice split the burgeoning night. "Tekeli-li. Tekeli-li."

Above, the factory's neon sign stirred to life, flashing in danger orange. Inside, track lighting kicked on. Three windows away the Husk loomed. From between drapes of oily black hair her maw flared wide, jaw muscles little more than stringy sinew. An over two-foot long 'tongue' flared out, repeatedly singing foreign syllables. The putty-like length merely palpitated out each sound, for it had no mouth of its own. A single eye drifted through the meaty muck, surfaced at the tendril's tip to stare at the children. It was hard to tell which was covered with more rancid ocher spots, her chalky skin or moldering black dress. Finger-sized pseudopodia writhed and stretched through those brown breaks in the shoggoth-slug's pilfered pelt. Sheer gauze floated away from somber skirts so riddled with holes it was easy to see ran stockings underneath. One foot was bare, the other wore a witchy-poo boot.

"Oh, God. Come on!" Nate didn't freeze up like his sister. He forcefully dragged her across the balcony.

The Husk didn't waste any time. She slid fluidly out the window and into tainted water. As she did so the unholy invertebrate coiled back into the safety of rotted gums. The stolen body rapidly cut through the water by undulating like an anaconda.

Nate threw the door open wide. Lindsey whimpered as he shoved her in and followed. The slight girl barely caught herself against the hand-rail instead of tumbling down the stairs. Her brother slammed the door shut and wished he had something to jam it up. He ignored his sister's pained squeak as he wrenched her by the arm and hurried upstairs.

"You're hurting me." She trembled, but didn't pull away. Nate didn't let up on the pace either. Their sprint fell staccato on metal stairs. They ran as hard as their small legs could carry them. Nate's lungs were burning; Lindsey's too.

Were the shoggoth older, bigger, it would have simply smashed through the door. Instead the Husk gingerly turned the handle as it had seen humans do and strutted onto the landing. She tipped her head back, sopping mop of hair plastered away from decaying features. A cluster of eyes seeped out of one cavernous socket, the other contained the convulsing tail of a fish being digested. The only sound the monster inside knew spilled out-- the bay of a hunting hound. The Husk took up after them. Overcome with anticipation she lost several fingers as a frenzy of feelers exploded out from the wrist. The fleshy bouquet of tendrils wrapped around the railing and helped pull her along.

Lindsey finally broke from her brother at the next landing. She reached for the door handle with both hands, gave it a hard jerk. Her already strained voice broke. "It's locked. It wasn't before!"

"Keep moving!"

The next floor and door produced the same results. The Husk keened 'Tekeli-li' so rapidly that it was almost cackling. The eye-socket once full of fish had crusted over with scabby meat. The siblings kept running. Both of them wanted nothing more than to sink down with exhaustion and accept this terrible fate, save that would mean abandoning the other. The tenth floor's door swung open when Nate pulled it, and both of them zipped into the litter-choked hall.

"Grab that chair!" The young man screamed.

Lindsey did as told and Nate wedged it against the door. Both knew that wouldn't hold the timeless terror. With any luck they'd bought themselves some breathing room. Not more than a moment was spared before they jogged down the hall. The pair kept stealing glances back, waiting for the door to shake. They were not disappointed. As soon as the knob jiggled the siblings broke into a run, or tried to anyway.

Without getting very far at all Nate took a tumble over a stray mop bucket and smashed to the floor. He didn't linger there long, springing back to his feet with youthful vigor. The pain would have to wait until later. Lindsey stopped, though, and fussed over him. Together they hurriedly maneuvered through the spilled contents of a fully-stocked janitor's closet. The girl snatched up a mop, because for someone her age it seemed a sensible weapon. Nate too looked for something he might use and chose a crusty box with a dead-cartoon mouse on the front. Maybe rat poison would slow the witch down? It was worth a try.

"Where are we going?" Lindsey asked when they were on the move again. As they darted around a corner the door finally gave away far behind them.

At first the young fellow considered ducking into the first room they came across and hiding. He didn't think they'd be able to escape the Husk with such a tactic a second time. His gaze caught an askew sign pointing toward roof access. "The roof. Come on. There's got to be a way down from there. Maybe, it won't follow us."

The pair pressed on. They had to round another two corners and navigate overturned vending machines filled with the company's candies. All the while the hollowed woman's chanting closed in. Nate felt like his body was going to give out at any moment, but he couldn't fail for Lindsey's sake. The boy paused at the bottom of rusty rungs, slowly looked up. The hatch was wide open. He could see starry night framed by distressed metal.

"Hurry!" Lindsey prodded him in the lower back. After a listless grunt hurry was exactly what Nate did. The box of coumarins ended up in his back pocket. The ascent was agonizingly slow.

When Nate got to the top, to his horror his sister wasn't even a third of the way up. She still carried the damned mop. He shot her a stern look and she thrust the weathered implement up to him. Once it was taken off of her hands Lindsey scurried and not a moment too soon! The Husk crouched atop a tipped snack machine. The monster inside watched little legs disappear through the hole.

The children closed the trap door, and then quickly looked for some place to hide. There was a sun-dried corpse propped against a length of vents – tell-tale self-inflicted wound and empty revolver evident. Neither Nate nor Lindsey batted an eye as rhythmic orange light pulsated and cleaved long shadows across the rooftop.

"Come on." Lindsey took her meager weapon and slid under the dented ductwork. Nate didn't follow. He knew he'd never fit, and needed to catch his breath. He hobbled as quickly as he could out of sight. He thought, incorrectly, the Husk wouldn't know where they were. Instead of cover he came across a fast-spinning fan recessed in the roof. Steam seeped from it, along with heat from industrial ovens. Humanity was all but gone, yet everything automated remained. He blinked slowly, savoring the warmth on his face, mesmerized by the spinning blades.

Nate felt Lindsey sneak up behind him. "We could just jump in you know, get it over with."

The boy realized the presence was not his sister when it leaned over his shoulder. A sickly sweet smell invaded his nostrils. The next sound was a mere whisper. "Tekeli-li."

Nate whirled and came face to membrane with the

Husk's central tentacle. The dead woman's head had split away like a banana peel, bloodlessly so. Dozens of glassy eyes clustered with luminescent green polyps pierced his gaze. The ocular spheres floated languidly away from a ripple in their center. It was from that ripple that a toothy mouth spread wide.

"I just want to go home." Nate whined, staring down the throatless maw.

The Husk buckled as Lindsey rammed the encrusted mop-head into the small of her back. While the encased shoggoth arched bonelessly her stolen skin proved the Husk's undoing. Using all the force she could muster, along with a loud roar, Lindsey managed to shove the atrocity away from her brother and past the lip of the vent. There wasn't even a scream as the fiend was rapidly diced. Her still wiggling chunks plummeted down the shaft to be baked, and then stuffed with crème filling that never expired.

Lindsey tossed the mop away and wrapped her arms around Nate. The pair quivered against one another, crying in relief for several minutes. As fear retreated fatigue set in, hunger returned. Lindsey was the first to speak. "Can we eat some cookies now?"

"Okay." Nate smoothed a hand over her pale ringlets. "Cookies sound great."

The pair jumped when a boat horn blared. It was followed by a spotlight cutting across the rooftop. The bright beam quickly found the embracing children. The horn bellowed again, and was joined by distant shouts. A cutter sliced gingerly through the water toward them, careful of toppled buildings but ignorant of what lay beneath.

"Papa! That's Papa's ship!" Tears sprung from the girl's bloodshot eyes. She let go of her brother and sprinted to the edge. She frantically flailed her arms in the air. "He's found us! He's alive. It's a miracle!"

Nate followed her example, but for completely different reasons. "Go back!" He screamed as loud as his small lungs could manage. "Stay away! For the love... of... God..."

All around the salvage vessel the water grew darker, as if a massive bottle of ink had spilled. The surface remained deceptively placid as the massive amoeba which prowled this sunken industrial zone floated up. The ship's crew received no warning. They were too focused on the waving children to notice the leprous illumination of its hundreds of hungry eyes. Sticky appendages inched up the side of the vessel. Lindsey screamed until she went shrill, curled her fists to her eyes, and smashed her face to Nate's chest. It was all over distressingly quick. The ship folded in the center like a pop can being crushed, save the treat inside was around thirty human souls. Their screams were quickly muffled as the titanic protoplasm engulfed the vessel. Ocean water splashed hard against the surrounding tops of submerged buildings as the cutter was violently pulled under. The spotlight sputtered out.

All was silent.

Save one weeping girl.

Nate wrapped his arms around her and stared at the still water. He had rat poison in his pocket and prepackaged cookies downstairs. "Everything is going to be okay."

About the Authors

Brent Abell

Brent Abell resides in Southern Indiana with his wife, sons, and a pug who rides on the mists of dreams and nightmares. He works full time, but has found time to be published in or have tales coming out from multiple presses and eZines. *In Memoriam*, his debut novella was released in October 2012 from Rymfire Books. You can hang out with him for some rum, a cigar, and all the latest news at http://brentabell.wordpress.com.

Twitter: @BrentTAbell
Facebook: Our Darkest Fears - The Fiction of Brent Abell

Vincent Bivona

Vincent Bivona is the genre-hopping author of 7 novels, including the award-winning novella *The Journal of Peter Rubin*, which is being taught in several universities and high schools throughout the United States. As long as you keep reading, he promises to keep writing.

Shenoa Carroll-Bradd

Shenoa Carroll-Bradd lives in Southern California with her brother and dancing dog. She writes whatever catches her fancy, from fantasy to horror and erotica.

Twitter: @ShenoaSays
Blog: www.sbcbfiction.net

Timothy C. Hobbs

Timothy Hobbs' novels *The Pumpkin Seed*, *Music Box Sonata*, *Maiden Fair* and a novella *The Smell of Ginger* are available from Amazon.com. A collection of his flash and short fiction, 'In the Blink of a Wicked Eye', is due for publication by Sirens Call Publications.

Kerry G.S. Lipp

Kerry teaches English at a community college by evening and writes horrible things by night. He hates the sun. His parents started reading his stories and now he's out of the will. Kerry's work appears in *DOA2* and *The Best of Cruentus Libri Press*.

Twitter: @kerrylipp
Facebook: - New World Horror - Kerry G.S. Lipp

Jon Olson

Aside from being a horror/dark fiction author, Jon also works full time as a Security Checkpoint Coordinator at the Halifax Robert L Stanfield International Airport. In 2007 he graduated from Saint Francis Xavier University obtaining his Bachelor of Arts degree in History. While he mainly writes short and flash fiction, he recently completed his first novella and also hopes to branch out to do some work in comics/graphic novels. When he is not writing or working, he can be found at his home in Eastern Passage, Nova Scotia with his wife and four cats.

Twitter: @jonolsonauthor
Facebook: www.facebook.com/authorjonolson

Zachary O'Shea

Zachary O'Shea was born in the refinery belt of California and raised in the neon desolation of Nevada. When not avoiding one armed bandits and tourists he enjoys various activities: running, designing, and occasionally playing table-top RPGs, reading, writing, and eating out too often with great friends.

Twitter: @BoxofTeeth
Website: www.lastslicestudios.com

Connor Rice

Connor Rice is an author who specializes in southern themed horror and urban fantasy stories. This is his second short story and hopes to have his first book finished soon; he currently lives in Oklahoma City where he works as an Emergency Medical Technician.

Justin M. Ryan

Justin M. Ryan is an author of entertaining genre fiction with a particular interest in short stories, novels, and comic books. His works, blog, and social media links can be found on the web at:

Twitter: @JustinMRyan87
Blog: justinmryan.com

SL Schmitz

One of these days, SL Schmitz is going to go to Loch Ness and swim with Nessie. Until then—she's going to continue writing bizarre, mythpunkian, irrational words that unravel all over the furniture and make a mess on the carpet.

Twitter: @SL_Schmitz
Website: www.slschmitz.com

Blaise Torrance

Blaise Torrance was born in Northern England and has since moved to Nottingham where she currently works in mental health services. Her short stories have been published in a number of small press anthologies. When not working or writing, she enjoys foil fencing, climbing and video games.

Patrick Van Slyke

Patrick Van Slyke grew up in the shadows of the Big Horn Mountains in the small town of Sheridan Wyoming. An avid reader, as a child he was drawn to fantasy and science fiction. He attended the University of Wyoming and it was here that his love of Horror began.

Twitter: @pvanslyke1
Facebook: www.facebook.com/patrickcvanslyke